ALL
THROUGH
THE DAY

Guy H. King

ALL
THROUGH
THE DAY

Meditations from the
Twenty-third Psalm

**ZONDERVAN
PUBLISHING HOUSE** OF THE ZONDERVAN CORPORATION
GRAND RAPIDS, MICHIGAN 49506

ALL THROUGH THE DAY
Copyright by Church Book Room Press,
London, England. First published in 1948.

1980 Zondervan Edition
published by special arrangement
with Vines Books, Ltd.,
London, England

Library of Congress Cataloging in Publication Data
King, Guy Hope.
   All through the day.

   (Christian classic series)
    1. Bible.   O.T.   Psalms XXIII—Meditations.
I. Title.   II. Series.
BS1450 23d .K56 1980   223'.2077   80-24448
ISBN 0-310-41831-3

Printed in the United States of America

CONTENTS

To my friend Alfred St. John Thorpe (Canon of St. Albans), a great under-shepherd, as I know through trying, at a great distance, to follow him at Christ Church, Beckenham: with esteem and affection.

PREFACE

The publishers asked me to write for them a devotional volume. Here it is, a series of studies based on the so familiar, but ever fresh, Shepherd Psalm. Alas, it has had to be written on my so-called holiday, so please deal gently with its many imperfections. As I wrote, under a sense of the spiritual sublimity of the subject, I felt like John Milton, at the beginning of his *Paradise Lost* —

> "What is dark in me illumine,
> What is low raise and support,
> That, to the height of this great argument,
> I may assert eternal providence,
> And justify the ways of God to men."

His are a Shepherd's ways, of unsleeping providence. May the Good Shepherd set His seal on the meditations of His sheep.

G.H.K.

Christ Church Vicarage,
Beckenham.
August, 1947.

The Twenty-third Psalm

The LORD is my shepherd; I shall not want.

²He maketh me to lie down in green pastures: he leadeth me beside the still waters.

³He restoreth my soul: he leadeth me in the paths of righteousness for his name's sake.

⁴Yea, though I walk through the valley of the shadow of death, I will fear no evil: for thou art with me; thy rod and thy staff they comfort me.

⁵Thou preparest a table before me in the presence of my enemies: thou anointest my head with oil; my cup runneth over.

⁶Surely goodness and mercy shall follow me all the days of my life: and I will dwell in the house of the LORD for ever.

Chapter One

ALL THROUGH THE DAY

This familiar and deeply loved psalm gives to us, I think, a typical day in the life of a sheep; and that is why I have chosen the title *All Through the Day*. But I have a feeling that, before setting out on my exposition, I ought to try to justify my attitude; for I know, of course, that by no means everyone will accept the view that I have here adopted. Some hold that three figures are employed by the psalmist to portray God's providential care for His people: that verses 1–2 present Jehovah as the Shepherd; verses 3–4 show Him as the Guide; and verses 5–6 picture Him as the Host. Others, however, aver that we have here two portrayals: the Shepherd, 1–4, and the Host, 5–6. A third school, of whom I am a humble disciple, believes that here is but one portrait, consistent throughout—that of the Shepherd, from the first verse to the last.

Let it be said again that this latter interpretation does not command the assent of all the commentators. In fact, the late Dr. J. D. Jones was quite nasty about it: "This reference to morning, afternoon and evening can only be secured by forced interpretation and by reading into the verses ideas which to the plain man do not appear to be there at all. I think we had better disregard all such explanations altogether as being artificial and purely imaginative." On the other hand, the late Dr. W. Y. Fullerton said, "The author of the psalm was too good an artist to change his simile midway, and if he was not, the Spirit who inspired him gave us a consistent picture . . . In the Twenty-third Psalm you have a picture of the whole day. Once you get hold of the clue it is impossible to miss it." After all, the guest of that exquisite little brochure, "The Song of our Syrian Guest," was evidently on intimate terms with the ways of eastern shepherds and sheep, and was hardly likely in such a field to be misled in commending to us this thought that the psalm takes us, stage by stage, through the sheep's day. By the way, Godet has the suggestion that we have the same thing in John 10—that Psalm 23 of the New Testament, even as the psalm is the John 10 of the Old Testament. Verses 1–6, says the distinguished French commentator, give us a morning picture; verses 7–10 are an afternoon scene; and verses 11–18 have an evening air about them.

There is nothing in the psalm to tell us positively who wrote it. The title itself is not inspired and was added at a much later date. Yet are we not in warm agreement with the late Dr. F. B. Meyer when he said, "There is no question as to who wrote it; David's autograph is on every verse"? John Freeman speaks of "this perfect lyric of religious trust, a lyric which has sung itself into the hearts of a thousand generations." Well, David was on the human side a beautifully accomplished poet. Besides, in early days he had been a shepherd and knew all there was to know about sheep and their daily needs. In fact, his experiences were so exciting, as in 1 Samuel 17:34–36, that the King on his throne must often have found himself daydreaming of humbler times. Be it said, however, that the psalm is written out of deep experience—no youth could have penned such words, no sheltered life could have given us such deep thoughts. It is a David in old age looking back on his times in the valley of dark shadow that writes these lines—a man who had been hunted by Saul, haunted by sin; and yet a David who, on thus looking back, realized how wondrously God had protected and provided and prospered him through it all. On all counts it seems indubitable that David is our author here.

So close is it to our own personal experience, and so provocative of our own individual testimony, that John McNeill quizzically said, "Fact is, I sometimes feel I wrote it myself." "The sweet words of the psalm," says Alexander Maclaren, "are not to be confined to material good. The psalmist does not tell us whether he is thinking more of the outer or of the inner life, but both are in his mind." And such has ever been the conviction of the multitude of souls that have drawn comfort, peace and inspiration from the glowing words.

The psalm stands as centerpiece in a remarkable trilogy. In Psalm 22 the theme is the Cross of the Savior—the Good Shepherd giving His life for the sheep; in Psalm 23 is the Crook of the Shepherd—the Great Shepherd girding and guarding and guiding and goading the sheep; in Psalm 24 is the Crown of the Sovereign—the Chief Shepherd returning to reign, and rewarding the sheep. It was of the first two that C. H. Spurgeon once said, "He who so lately bewailed the woes of the Shepherd, tunefully rehearses the joys of the flock." Remember how Zechariah 13:7 says, "Awake, O sword [the sword of Divine justice] against my shepherd"; yes, and Hebrews 13:20 telling of how God "brought again from the dead . . . that great shepherd of the sheep." The true "sheep of His hand," as Psalm 95:7 describes them, can never, never forget how stained with blood and scarred with wound was that hand stretched out to rescue them, nor how alive with resurrection power is that hand reached out to succor and sustain them.

It is truly remarkable how full and frequent are the references throughout the Bible to the shepherd-ministry of God. They say, though I have not checked the figure, that sheep, lambs and shepherds are mentioned 1,140 times. Likewise, as Dr. Fullerton has told us, "the thought of the Lord as the Shepherd was more constantly before the early church than any other. They knew that they needed His care, and they believed that they had it. If you have been privileged to walk along the Catacombs you will remember that nearly always the Lord is pictured as the Shepherd." Truly it is a thought that has ever been precious to those who have suffered in His name. Those who were present at it will never forget a meeting held under the auspices of the ever-beloved China Inland Mission in the great Central Hall in London, when, for fifty heart-gripping minutes, Mr. R. A. Bosshardt told something of the experiences of his eighteen months' captivity and of his torture at the hands of Chinese Communists, and how, at the close of the meeting the vast assembly with scarce a dry eye in the place sang the sweet children's hymn:

> *Jesus is our Shepherd, wiping every tear;*
> *If we love and trust Him, what have we to fear?*

On the other side of the picture, however, it clamors to be said that it is no flattery that the Bible likens us to sheep. How attractive they look in our still-life Christmas cards; how fascinating as we see them out of the window of a hurrying railway train—those gamboling youngsters, those docile oldsters! Yes: but, do you know anything about sheep? Ask Moses! For forty years at the Egyptian Court he had learned to be somebody; but at the end of another forty years he had learned to be nobody and was constrained to inquire "Who am I . . . ?" (Exod. 3:11). What had wrought so amazing a change? This, perhaps: for that second term of years he was mostly engaged in minding sheep! They are such silly and contrary creatures that they are guaranteed to teach anyone his sheer nothingness. "Like sheep," says Isaiah 53:6, about us—yet, for all that, how blissful it is when that wandering sheep is found and is entitled to look up into his Savior's face and say "My Shepherd," and when his enravished heart hears His loving voice say "My sheep."

Pause there for a moment while I say that there are, alas, some who pass among their fellows for saved sheep while, in reality, they are but washed swine. You must have heard the legend of the Chinese Emperor's little pet pig. He had, from its birth, brought it up to be so completely different from all others of its ilk. It was daily washed, and beautifully clothed, and faddishly fed—all piggish tastes and habits were eradicated from its nature. Often, on a lead, it would accompany its Imperial Master on his walks abroad, the little pet the delight of passers-by. One day, while thus linked together they happened to be at a place where, in the near distance, was an evil muddy puddle. All of a sudden there was a sniff and a snort, there was a violent tug at the unprepared leash and the perfect little gentleman was off! Before they could stop it, it was rolling in the mud: its pig's heart hadn't been changed. A stupid tale; but a solemn truth. Many, I say again, appear to be sheep who are swine still; and when they slip back into evil ways people mistakenly refer to them as backsliders when, as a matter of fact, they never were Christians at all; spectators look criticizingly on and sneeringly observe that these "results" never last, when, in truth, they have never actually begun. As 2 Peter 2:22 says, "It is happened unto them according to the true proverb, The dog is turned to his own vomit again; and the sow that was washed to her wallowing in the mire." You see, my illustration is a scriptural one; and it behooves us all to make quite sure that we are indeed His sheep before we pass on to think over what it means to have His shepherding care. It is time now that we turned to that grand theme as unfolded for us in the wonderful psalm.

My friend, Mr. Lindsay Glegg, is fond of telling the story of how one evening in an hotel lounge a company of men were talking when the conversation turned to the subject of declaiming pieces of great literature. A famous actor was present and by way of example he recited the Twenty-third Psalm—with perfect enunciation, modulation and expression. It was beautifully done. There was also present a quiet, benign old clergyman. He followed with the same psalm—also, in his own way, beautifully done. The comment afterwards of one of the group was, "The actor knows the Shepherd Psalm, but the clergyman knows the Shepherd." Well—it is my prayer that our present study of this poetic gem of inspiration may lead some to come to know Him for the first time, and lead us all to get to know Him better and better, until we too come to "dwell in the house of the LORD for ever."

Chapter Two

THE EARLY MORNING START

"The LORD *is my shepherd; I shall not want. He maketh me to lie down in green pastures: he leadeth me beside the still waters."*

Oh, yes, the sheep's day begins early: would that the day of all of us Christians did likewise. Some are so placed and circumstanced that it is not possible; but most of us could, if we would, arrange to begin our day with that early morning quiet time for God, which proves so precious to those who practice it. Is it not a striking thing that almost, if not quite, without exception all those who have done great work for God have had this godly habit? I am greatly impressed with that word which God spoke to Moses in Exodus 34:2, "Be ready in the morning." What a grand rule of life that would be for any Christian! If thus we get in touch with God as the day opens, the succeeding hours will be rightly adjusted whatever experiences they may hold. So, in the early morning, the sheep begins his day.

All Through the Day

"When I awake I am still with thee," said this same psalmist (139:18). The night before he had committed himself to God as he lay down to sleep, and now the morning's dawning finds him in the same blessed presence. Just so is it with this sheep. His first waking thought is, "The LORD is my Shepherd," even as his last conscious thought had been. A visitor to Palestine was once being shown over the hills by a native of the country who pointed out a lonely sheepfold—just four bare, high walls, with an opening in the one. "But where is the door?" asked the guest; to which the reply was given that if he were there at eventide, he would see the flock ushered into their resting-place, and then at nightfall the shepherd would lie in that vacant space and be himself the door. A shepherd is by custom a very light sleeper; and any intruding foe would have first to reckon with him. How suggestively reminiscent of our Good Shepherd who, in John 10:7, said, "I am the door." The sheep's last reassuring sight was the form of the shepherd in the doorway; and now he opens his eyes to the first, fresh vision of the morning, and lo, it is the same fair form at his side, "The LORD is my Shepherd." All through the night He had watched over him; and now, all through the day, He will be with him. What a thought, what a fact, to begin the day with! He knows not what the day holds in store for him; but he knows that it will hold Him—and that is enough!

For, *Who is this Shepherd?* It is "the LORD"—printed in our Bibles in small capital letters and being, therefore, the translation of the Divine Name Jehovah: the True God. What a truly wonderful thing it is that, as soon as a soul believes on Him, all the attributes of deity are on his side! *(a) His Omniscience*—knowing all about His sheep, their individual condition and circumstances, their individual weaknesses and needs, the things that are for their individual welfare, and how to bring those things to pass. What peace we draw from this divine quality! *(b) His Omnipresence*—that wherever His sheep are He is ever by the side of all of them and of each of them, so that this one and that one, beloved to each other though separated far from each other, are never separated from Him, and both are, whether at home or in foreign lands, whether here or in the Glory, enjoying the same presence at the same moment, even this very moment. What joy is ours in the realization of that divine quality! *(c) His Omnipotence*—that what His love wants is the best for us, and what His wisdom knows to be that best for us, His power can procure and produce for His sheep; and that provided His hands are not tied as, alas, they can be by our sins (Isa. 59:1–2); or by our compromise (Gen. 19:22); or by our unbelief (Mark 6:5–6). There is no limit to what His almightiness can do for us if He so will. What security grips our hearts as we contemplate this further divine quality! *(d) His Omniexistence*—that He abides ever, and ever the same; that the God who lived in Abram's time and in Moses' time and in Daniel's time, is just the same today, unchangeably the same, always the invariable "I Am"; that our psalm has not said, "The Lord *was* David's Shepherd," but, "the LORD *is* my Shepherd." What gladness fills my heart at the recollection of such a divine quality when I turn to the inspired record of His dealings with the old Bible worthies and when I read what He has done for, and been to, His saints all down the ages since, and understand that He is ready to be just such even to me also.

But, *What is our relationship with this Shepherd?* We return to press the point of a previous page. "My"—what a word it is; and what condescending grace that allows us to claim possession of Him as our own! Can we so do? Some years ago a certain church in a town in Derbyshire was holding its Sunday school anniversary when the local member of Parliament, a godless man, was induced to attend. Something happened to him at that service which completely altered his whole life and future. Let me once more (for almost every preacher has told the story, or at least the first part of it—the Scotch part; though the Derbyshire part is almost unknown) recount the familiar tale. The preacher that day said that a man taking his holiday in Scotland came upon a shepherd boy in a field minding the flock. Sitting down beside him the stranger presently asked him if he knew the Twenty-third Psalm. Of course he did: he was a Scotch boy! "Then, what is the opening sentence?" "The LORD is my Shepherd." "Say it again now, ticking off a finger for each word." "The — LORD — is — my — Shepherd." Then came some earnest words from the Christian man explaining how, by definitely accepting Him as our Savior and Lord, we can have Him for our own. There and then in that field on that lovely quiet summer morning the lad did for himself "receive" Him (John 1:12); and before the two separated, the shepherd-boy said the words over again, finger by finger, this time clutching hard at the fourth. "The — LORD — is — MY — Shepherd." The succeeding winter was a severe one; and it so happened that one day the snow had fallen very heavily, and neither the boy nor his sheep came home—they were all caught and buried in a deep drift. When they came to dig, they discovered the bodies of many dead sheep, and presently they came on the wee laddie—quite dead, lying on his back, peace on his face, the fourth finger of his left hand grasped by his right hand. Such was his last thought and such his hope for eternal years. That was the story the preacher told in the Derbyshire church that day, which deeply impressed the godless M.P. And the sequel? That immediately, the man was quite changed in outlook and behavior giving evidence that something had happened inside; and some years later the man died in his bed, and when they turned down the sheet they found his right hand holding the fourth finger of his left. Come now, will you, as in His presence, put this book down for a moment, and will you—if you are so entitled—do as was done those days by boy and man?

Oh, the difference that *"my"* makes! A little group of boys were discussing a pocket-knife that was being passed around among them. One boy said, "What a lovely knife"; another said, "What an expensive knife"; a third said, "What a useful knife"; a fourth, "What a sharp knife" as each passed it longingly along. As it came back to the last boy in the circle, he said, "Yes, it's *my* knife!" So he was in the fortunate position of being able to enjoy all its values for himself. Oh yes, and John 10:14 says He is "the good shepherd"; and Hebrews 13:20 says He is "that great shepherd"; and 1 Peter 5:4 says He is "the chief shepherd"; all so wonderfully and gloriously true, but Psalm 23:1 says He is *"my* shepherd"—the One Who has suffered for me and sought me and saved me and satisfied me and sheltered me and so much else!

So then our sheep, that early morning, is awake to the Shepherd's presence; but more, He is—

AWARE OF THE SHEPHERD'S CARE

"I shall not want." Says Psalm 34:10, "the young lions" do want; but not the young sheep! They "shall not want any good thing." And Psalm 84:11 backs that up by saying that "no good thing will He withhold from them that walk uprightly." So we may be quite sure that if any greatly desired thing is withheld, the reason for the "lack" is either that we are not walking uprightly or else that it is not really a "good thing" for us: good in general, perhaps, or good for somebody else, but not good for us. That is clear, isn't it?

It is good to start out in the morning with the assurance in my heart that "I shall not want." Such a conviction gives peace and poise to any life, whether the words be taken materially or spiritually. We think of *(a) The Variety of our Need*—perhaps our psalm may be said to suggest three words that summarize it: food, foes and future; our ever recurring necessity for provision, for protection, and for progression. And over against all that, we think of *(b) The Sufficiency of His Supply*—as the psalm will gradually unfold. It is blessedly true concerning each step of the way, concerning each stage of the day, that "I shall not want" because supply and demand, demand and supply, exactly coincide.

The other day I found myself hanging pictures; and I discovered, as always, that the problem was not what pictures to use, but in what order to place them. It is so important that in form, and in color, and in treatment they blend, each matching each. Go to that picture-gallery of a verse which we know as Philippians 4:19 and stand before that almost infinitely varied canvas "Your Need"—what a problem picture it is, what a complexity of detail is in it, what a large sweep of execution it displays, what an almost overpowering effect it has on you, its very size weighs down your spirit! Hanging there on the wall by itself it would greatly depress you. But look! There is another alongside it—"My God." A vast canvas, filled with such immensities as are quite beyond our capacity to take in—a picture at once of exquisite beauty and of enormous power. That first picture seems now to look smaller by comparison, doesn't it? But wait, there's a third, "His Riches"—an exact companion of that other large one. Here is a life-like presentment that looks for all the world like an inexhaustible gold mine, with a wealth of priceless jewels scattered, as if carelessly, besides. The price of everything within this world and beyond would seem to be adequately covered within the compass of this grand conception. Yet stay: what has happened to that picture we first examined? Has it grown smaller? No; it is as big as ever, "Your Need"—it only looks smaller as hung between those other two. That is the way to hang the three and that way will give us the true balance between them. Let us not forget that the picture of our need will never become so big as to outgrow those of our God and of His riches. Truly "I shall not want."

Or, go to 1 Peter. There, in 1:6, and in 4:10, the apostle uses a very interesting Greek word that occurs nowhere else in the New Testament. In both places it is translated "manifold." The first is, "manifold temptations," or trials, testings: how vast, and how varied, was the need they created in those persecution days of the early church; and, though different in character and in degree in these days of the modern church, yet they are many enough and menacing enough still. How shall they be met? Peter answers in his second place, "Manifold grace"—always the particular kind of grace to match the particular kind of need. Just now, in the "My" story, we were doing a five finger exercise. Will you do another one? This time let the fingers of your left hand stand for your "manifold" tests and needs—all so different: a great thumb of a need, a differing size of needs, a little bit of a need. Now, let the fingers of your right hand represent the "manifold" covering of God's grace—a big thumb grace, a differing sized grace, a little grace: each finger of grace made exactly to fit and completely to meet each finger of need. Truly, "I shall not want."

Oh, I know that, from another angle, we are a bundle of wants; and, as John McNeill says, "a bundle badly tied and bursting the string"—wants of body and mind, wants of home and business, wants of work and play, wants of this life and the next, wants of time and eternity. The psalmist would say, "I have wants; but I shall not want." If we may put it so: want as a noun he will always know, but want as a verb he will never know. That is his claim here. Have you noticed that sheep are the most placid of animals? They never worry! Instead, they have the most implicit trust in the shepherd.

Doubtless there are some who question, as they read, whether such a claim can really be substantiated in respect of physical and material things. "I shall not want." But, says someone, I do want; my experience is quite contrary to the psalmist's statement. Dr. F. B. Meyer, a man who knew the necessities and problems of life if ever a man did, believed that David's assurance held good in the material realm, and he said that if our experience seemed to contradict that it was probably due to one or other of four reasons—(1) we have not by faith sought and appropriated the supplies which have been placed ready to our hand; (2) we have not made our requests known to God with prayer and supplication; (3) our hour of need has not yet fully come; or (4) we have misunderstood our real need, and are asking for something which would do us harm. On the other hand how many and how heartening are the glad testimonies of God's people who, ordering their lives in accordance with His will, have found in day by day experience that He does take care of those who obey Him and trust Him. I love those words of Leslie Weatherhead's: "After all, Jesus taught men to pray definitely for bread, not merely that if starving they might bear the pangs of hunger with greater fortitude."

And so this early morning his heart rejoicing in His presence, his mind resting in the certainty of His care, the sheep is—

Away Under the Shepherd's Lead

"He maketh me to lie down in green pastures: he leadeth me beside the still waters." John 10:4 tells us that "when He putteth forth His own sheep, He goeth before them, and the sheep follow Him: for they know His voice." That is in accordance with eastern practice, which is the reverse of our way. Their shepherds lead, while ours drive, the sheep. I have heard the Rev. L. T. Pearson, a great authority on Palestinian and Syrian matters, tell of a visitor to the Holy Land who was on one occasion greatly surprised to come upon an exception to this rule—this shepherd was actually driving his sheep. He went and spoke to the man, and said that he understood that an eastern shepherd always led his sheep. "Bless you," was the reply, "I'm not a shepherd, I'm a butcher!"

The sheep follow because they know their shepherd's voice. In a mountainside sheepfold there will probably be several different flocks that have sheltered there for the night all mixed up together; and it is a fascinating thing to stand and watch what happens in the early morning as they start out on their day's journey. First, one shepherd will make his call, and instantly "his own sheep" will separate themselves from the rest and come out to him, "for they know his voice"; then another will sound his call with the same result; until at last, all the flocks are on their way. There is never any mistake. The same separating magic is seen when, flock by flock, the shepherds call their charges from the wells of water. By the way, if you were to take a hand in this business and, having learned his call from one of those shepherds, were to try it on the sheep, not one of them would take any notice of you except perhaps to blink an eyelid (we call it winking) as if to say, "We're not going to be caught that way." You see, "they know not the voice of strangers." Oh, that we might be so intimate with our Divine Shepherd that we shall always instinctively recognize His voice, and that we may be so obedient to Him that we shall instantly follow His lead!

Perhaps it will not be without profit if we take a moment or two to consider some of the ways in which God gives us His leading and guidance, for it is often one of a Christian's biggest problems to know how to discover what is God's will for him. Do you know, I wonder, that remarkable typical chapter on guidance, Numbers 10? A careful study of it would prove very rewarding. Just now, we can only indicate the points. We are told there that Israel was to find God's guidance for their wilderness journeyings in four ways (1) *The Trumpets* picture His Word, the two instruments representing the two testaments.

To get the guidance of the Bible requires a day by day diligence in its study, so that we shall gradually come to know almost instinctively what its teaching would be on a given matter. Not by shutting our eyes, opening at random, thrusting a pin haphazard, and taking the verse as leading, shall we know its secret. All that might be very appropriate for a fortuneteller's antics, but not for Christian guidance seekers. As we steep our minds in the Word we shall find that over and over again our message will come to us with trumpet-like clarity. (2) *The Cloud* pictures His Spirit, who is appointed for this age to "guide you into all [the] truth" (John 16:13), and who is so ready to give us our lead if we are as ready to follow it when given. Incidentally, it will be found that the cloud is never at variance with the trumpets. (3) *The Father-in-law* pictures His servants, who, like Hobab, have had long experience of the wilderness and could give good advice in problems that arise and as it were, "be to us instead of eyes." God will often bring His guidance to us by sending us to consult with some experienced Christian who knows the way and can, out of ripe knowledge, give sound counsel. Let us not forget that any experience of life that we may have acquired is meant, among other things, to equip us for the ministry of guiding others in the way. (4) *The Ark* pictures His Son, the Lord Jesus, in whom rests the unbroken Law. We have to guide us the record of His words and ways; from what He said and did we can draw the inference of what He would say and do in our present circumstances, and so "follow His steps" (1 Peter 2:21). By these and other means He instructs us in the way in which we should go.

And where will our following take us? To *"green pastures"*—that is, pastures of tender grass. Down in the valley there will be plenty of coarse grass, eminently suitable for goats; but sheep need the more succulent provender of the hillside. This is by no means plentiful and has to be diligently sought. I don't know how it is today, but some years ago it was computed that there were something like four million sheep in the Holy Land, so that the shepherds had their work cut out to find "green pastures" for their flocks. The Good Shepherd leads us to the ever fresh pasturage of the Word, where there is always "food convenient" for us (Prov. 30:8) and that in rich abundance. "Fresh" did I say? Yes, always fresh. Those of you who have read the late Sir Ernest Shackleton's enthralling book *South* will recall the incident of the party that went off planting depots for future use. All went well until they turned home for base. Three of the six men went desperately ill and presently, what with frost-bite and scurvy, it developed for all six into a grim fight for life. In the diary of the leader one note constantly recurs: for example, "No mistake, it is scurvy, and the only possible cure is fresh food"; again, "If one could only get some fresh food." Well, thank God there is always fresh food for the Christian venturer in the green pastures of the Scriptures. Sometimes we come upon patches which are so gloriously up-to-date that it seems as if they must have been written but yesterday, and there's never a stale stretch anywhere: even the familiar Twenty-third Psalm seems new every time we come to it. Sometimes, alas, we are slack about our soul's meals; and then "He maketh me." Maybe we are too busy about other things; and be assured that if we are too busy to find time for Bible study, we are busier than He wants us to be—even though our many occupations are in Christian service. Or maybe by reason of those other things we have lost our appetite—the sweetmeats of worldly pleasures or even the tasty confectionery of exciting and emotional campaign meetings can so easily take away our taste for the regular solid food of the Word, and we become sickly and delicate sheep. But when we give serious attention to this feeding, we "grow thereby" (1 Peter 2:2).

During an instance of extraordinarily severe weather in the

British Isles, many sheep perished from sheer starvation; and it would seem that not a few of His sheep are starving themselves because they will not feed on the Word. It has before now happened that God has had to put His children on their backs in sickness, since only so would they take time to commune with Him, and only thus the "sheep look up, and are . . . fed." But that, of course, is not the real significance of our phrase, "He maketh me to lie down." The fact is, that sheep never lie down till they are well fed; and then they rest to digest their meal. Our Church of England's opening prayer asks that we may "hear, read, mark, learn and inwardly digest" the Holy Scriptures, or, as Joshua 1:8 puts it, that the soul's "mouth" having partaken of the portion we may "meditate therein." We may be quite sure that wherever else the Shepherd will lead His flock in that early morning hour, he will take them to the pasture of His Word, for He knows, as that other shepherd knows, the all-importance of nourishment and refreshment for the beginning of the day. "It is by a constancy of the means of grace," says Matthew Henry, "that the soul is fed."

And, as if to emphasize and underline the thought, our psalmist employs another figure to the same end—"the *still waters.*" Have you realized that in this country it is very unusual for sheep to drink? They normally acquire all the moisture they need from the pasturage, unless, in a very hot spell, everything gets dried up. In the East, however, it is all very different. In the summer it is so hot that the brooks and rivulets get completely emptied; and what in the rainy season was a mountain torrent becomes but a bed of hard, dry stones. But there are always the wells. All over these Judean hills there are deep walled wells, whose waters never fail. A good shepherd carries in his mind a chart of every well in his grazing area; and thither he turns the footsteps of his flock, where he will let down the bucket, and fill the trough with refreshing, sparkling water. "Still waters," you notice, for sheep will never drink of a rushing stream; turbulent waters frighten them, and some have even been drowned by essaying refreshment there. These latter are all very well for lions, but not for lambs. By the way, be careful lest by doing what will do you no harm, you lead a "weaker brother" to do the same thing to his harm. You may be a lion of a Christian, but remember that things that may be safe for you might be dangerous to a lamb of a Christian. Now in Bible symbols running waters are a type of the Holy Spirit but still waters are a type of the Holy Scriptures. So here we are once more back at the same theme—the essential importance at the opening day, of "the . . . water by the Word" (Eph. 5:26). Surely we shall learn afresh by this reiteration of emphasis to begin each early morning with this sweet and sustaining communion with our Lord.

This is but the beginning of His day's leadership; because otherwise the sheep will be "gone astray" (Isaiah 53:6) and become "lost" to His care (Luke 15:6) "they follow Him"—never usurping the leadership, content to tread in the track of so wise a Counselor and Guide. It is told of the late Professor D. S. Cairns that he had a rather pleasing habit, when passing with another through a door, a gate, or a passage-way, of stepping aside and saying to his companion, "You go first, I follow." The phrase was so common with him that it became associated with his name. After many years, as he lay dying, his lips were seen to be moving, and as they bent down to catch his words, they heard him say, "You go first, I follow." There was no doubt of the One to Whom the good old man was speaking that time: the Shepherd led and the sheep followed into "the pastures of the blest."

Chapter Three

THE NOON-TIDE HALT

"He restoreth my soul."

The sheep's siesta! In every walk of life it is plain to see that pause pays; resting time is not wasting time. Isn't that one of the great values of holidays—and of Sundays? During a discussion about whether the golf courses of Scotland should be opened on the Sabbath, an old green-keeper put in the argument that if the players didn't need a day of rest, the greens did! Have you heard about Mr. Winston Churchill's habit during all the pressure of his immense responsibilities during the War—indeed, I believe it has been almost a life-long custom of his—that every day, after lunch, he went to bed for three-quarters of an hour. All the world knows that that was not wasted time. So does the shepherd lead his flock to a break for quiet rest at midday. That means—

RELAXATION—BECAUSE THE NOON IS HERE

It is a time of tropic heat when everybody will, if possible, relax from all activity. Nothing more dramatically displays the infatuated and infuriated madness of Saul of Tarsus against Jesus and His disciples than the fact that he continued his pursuit "at midday," as he told Agrippa (Acts 26:13). His implacable hatred forbade him rest, even at such an hour. Even the sheep must rest in that great heat. The night has been cold with heavy frost, and the shepherd has been glad of his sheepskin to keep him warm; but the sun has soon changed all that. By noon its rays are burning with great intensity, and the shepherd has gathered his flock around him in some place where thick bushes, or high rocks, are throwing their shadow. How grateful the sheep are to have this still further evidence of their shepherd's knowledge of their need and of his provision for their comfort! They have noted that any bleat of distress brings him alongside at once, but now it is too hot even to bleat; yet, sure enough, there he is, interpreting their deepest longing, and satisfying their panting want.

It may, perhaps, be said that the sun of life is fiercest at the midway of the years—when difficulties abound, and resilience is feeblest, and temptation is hottest, and everything is a burden, and spirituality is at its lowest ebb. Then is the time to look for some cooling, restful shade.

When the sense of sin is burning within us, let us find our way to *the shadow of the Cross* where we shall ever find healing:

> *Beneath the Cross of Jesus I fain would take my stand,*
> *The shadow of a mighty rock within a weary land.*

When the spirit is fevered by the pressure of the all-too-obvious success of evil designs in the world, by the massing of the forces of wrong, let us turn to *the shadow of the Throne,* where the haze and maze of things are seen in true proportion, as we realize afresh that, in spite of all appearances—

> *God is still on the throne.*
> *And He will remember His own.*

"The LORD reigneth, let the people tremble," as Psalm 99:1 says.

When our heart is hot with the sense of our weakness, and ineffectiveness, and loneliness, let us make for *the shadow of the Man*, and hide in Him, for it is blessedly true that "a Man shall be . . . as the shadow of a great rock in a weary land" (Isa. 32:2). If it was true, as in Acts 5:15, that fevered bodies found healing in "the shadow of Peter," how much surer and deeper will be the ministry of the shadow of Him who, in Isaiah 26:4 (margin) is called "the Rock of Ages." Psalm 37:1–9 is a rare passage for fevered brows. Three times over it says "Fret not thyself" and they tell me that the Hebrew of the phrase is really "Don't get hot!" A counsel of perfection, did you say, amid the stress and strain of life's perplexing problems? Well, the Bible never tells us *what* without also telling us *how*; and here is no exception. For the verses point us away from the puzzles to the Person who can solve them—"Trust in the LORD" (v. 3); "Delight thyself in the LORD" (v. 4); "Commit thy way unto the LORD" (v. 5); "Rest in the LORD" (v. 7). This same Lord is ever ready to invite us to take shade in Himself; He says continually to us, as in different circumstances He said to Moses, "There is a place by me . . . upon a rock . . . in a clift of the rock" (Exod. 33:21–22)—yea, "cleft for me"! So shall it come happily to pass that in the shadow of the Cross, and the Throne, and the Man, we shall find heart's ease from the glare of the noon-day heat. When one thinks of "the destruction that wasteth at noon-day" (Psalm 91:6) one is not surprised at the psalmist's resolution, "Evening, and morning, and at noon will I pray" (Ps. 55:17).

During the 1914 War, when Lord Kitchener reigned at the War Office, he made a practice of breaking off from his arduous duties every day at noon, when, for a brief respite, he went to a nearby church, and there prayed. If that rather silent man had permitted himself to explain, he would doubtless have used some such words as those of our psalmist, "He restoreth my soul." Be it the heat of strong temptation, or of great prosperity, or of worrying care, the longing of our spirits will be—

> *Breathe through the heats of our desire*
> *Thy sweetness and Thy balm;*
> *Let flesh be dumb, let sense retire,*
> *Speak through the earthquake, wind, and fire,*
> *O still small voice of calm.*

So shall we bless God for the noon-day halt, and the relaxation it brings, the chance to let up for a bit, and to lean back on Him. Some doctors prescribe muscle relaxation for their overly tired patients—just to lie down and gradually let every muscle go limp. It takes some practice, we must acquire the art; and it had better be done when alone, for we shall not look our best during the exercise; but it can prove a rare boon. Soul relaxation, too, calls for practice and for privacy; but what a blessing it will prove in the scorching mid-day sun. The halt means further—

RECUPERATION—BECAUSE THE FORENOON IS BEHIND

Energies have been expended since that early start. *(a) The sheep has been going all the morning,* after its own fashion; its body is tired, it is glad of the rest. And certain it is that we Christians grow tired—in the work; but not of it. Or, are we so slack in our service that we never get exhausted? I have often seen businessmen tired in their work; I have often seen soldiers tired in their duty; I have often seen athletes tired in their sport; but I have not as often seen those engaged as Christian businessmen (Luke 19:13), or as Christian soldiers (2 Tim. 2:3), or as Christian athletes (1 Cor. 9:24) tired out with the strenuousness of their service. Alas, that so rarely we are "all in," because we are so seldom "all out." But those who so gladly spend and are spent in following Him, do so welcome His summons, "Come unto Me . . . and I will give you rest" (Matt. 11:28).

Moreover *(b) The sheep has, perhaps, been wandering*—and this may, possibly, be the particular point of the "restoring" here; for the Hebrew of the word really means to "bring back." Sheep, like ourselves, are prone to wander; but that is a very serious habit. Leslie Weatherhead says, "From some source which I cannot now trace, I have gathered that . . . there was an ancient law in Palestine which decreed that if an animal strayed from the care of its owner onto the land of another, and remained there over a proved period of one day, it could not be reclaimed by its original owner, but became the property of the one on whose land it was found." It would sometimes happen that a shepherd would break the leg of an habitual strayer to break it of the habit. Do you think that, just out of love to us, our Good Shepherd sometimes allows a break to come to us, some painful experience, in order to prevent our wandering from Him? It seems, too, that a man would deliberately trap a neighbor's sheep. He would dig a deep pit, cover it over with branches, and overlay them with turf. A sheep straying onto this treacherous surface would, of course, fall through and be trapped. Unless the owner found it within the specified time it could not be reclaimed. Hence the urgency of the law which allowed the rescue to be made even on the Sabbath day (Matt. 12:11). There must the poor frightened animal remain, for it cannot save itself, until its shepherd comes to lift it up and out—all it can do is to bleat its cry of distress. I expect David in his shepherd days had sometimes had to do this for one of his father's flock; and I have no doubt that his mind was on just such an experience when, in later days, he felt himself spiritually to have been in that sheep's evil case and wrote in Psalm 40:1–2, "I waited patiently for the LORD; and he inclined unto me, and heard my cry. He brought me up also out of an horrible pit."

Let it be noted that it is not the hearty feeders that wander, but the nibblers—going from tuft to tuft, after the delicacies of the pasture, getting further and further from the shepherd, nearer and nearer into danger. You will always find, in any flock, that the fattest sheep are those nearest the shepherd. Certainly that is true of the flock of Christ. There are all too many Christians running hither and thither after the spiritual delicacies—as they consider them—rushing after the gifted campaign leaders and feeding on their often most helpful addresses, restlessly discontented with the more solid provender of the home pastor; or happily browsing among the plethora of books about the Bible, some of them most delightful and illuminating, and having no real appetite for the Bible itself, giving no time to the solid study of it. No wonder these become poor, thin Christians having little strength to resist the force of temptation and pulling no weight in the life and work of their church; no wonder they are nervy, and irritable and fearful in the face of opposition, and in their relation with some of their fellow Christians. There would be far fewer wanderers if there were far fewer nibblers. And since wandering is so serious, and so perilous a matter, let us have done with faddy feeding and get on to the real "meat" of the Word, which according to 1 Corintians 3:1–3, would be a sure safeguard against that nervy condition that engenders strife.

So it comes to pass that *(c) The sheep is now called back*—in order to do which the shepherd will probably use his sling and stone. This becomes usually one of a shepherd's most expert accomplishments. While he is minding the flock, with little particular to do, he will practice and practice and practice, until he is adept enough to hit a small target at a long distance. In Eastern armies of those days, there were often regular corps of slingers: Judges 20:16 tells us of "seven hundred chosen men left-handed; every one could sling stones at an hair breadth and not miss." David had, by diligent cultivation, acquired that gift as we know from his using it to conquer the mighty Goliath in 1 Samuel 27:49. One little spot in all the giant's body was unarmoured, and the shepherd lad aimed at that point and with his first stone (though he had modestly chosen five) he hit. By the way, little do we know how any practiced gift can be used one day in the service of God; even the most unlikely accomplishment can be put to use for Him—music, painting, stamp-collecting, needlework, airplanes, sport, cookery, oh, almost anything: even slings and stones. The shepherd, then, would aim, not to hit the wanderer, but to land his stone just in front of its nose, causing it to look up startled: it would know what it meant and would quickly be finding its way back. Our Shepherd, too, has His own way of arousing our attention and fetching us back to rest with Him from the noon-day heat—some "smooth stone" chosen from the brook of the Book that "shall accomplish that . . . where to I sent it" (Isa. 55:11). Thus His message reaches us, bidding us return.

It was when their hearts were hot with indignation and sorrow, over the beheading of John the Baptist, that the Master said, "Come ye yourselves apart . . . and rest awhile" (Mark 6:31). So it is, and thus it is, that whether wandering in sin, or weakening in service, or wilting in self, "He restoreth my soul." The God-given halt, or breathing space, means one more thing—

REHABILITATION—BECAUSE THE AFTERNOON IS AHEAD

There lies ahead a certain round; it will not be haphazard, but will all be definitely planned by the shepherd. I feel that the same thing is true of every Christian's whole life; and every day God has a specific purpose, and a particular plan, for each of us. The secret is to place ourselves quite deliberately under His direction, telling Him that we want, for this one day, only His will and His program, and asking Him that, whether we be conscious of it or not, we may be led of Him, whatever we do, and wherever we go. As the morning opens, we may well make the psalmist's dual prayer in Psalm 119:33–35 our own: "Teach me the way . . . make me to go."

In planning for the afternoon *(a) The shepherd knows his sheep*—each one. Dr. Horace Bushnell reminds us that "the Lord is not the keeper of a hive of bees, knowing well the hive, but not knowing the individual bees; but is the keeper of a flock of sheep, knowing well the flock, but knowing also each particular sheep." To you they all look alike, but to the shepherd each animal is different, and, indeed, he has a nickname for each one—maybe, the name of a flower; or, perhaps, some little peculiarity: Blacknose, One-ear, Stump-tail, etc. Curiously enough, they all respond to their own name. How happily we remember, in John 10:3, that "He calleth his own sheep by name, and leadeth them out." Knowing them so well, he will not forget that they are not very robust animals; and (Ps. 103:14), "He knoweth our frame." Recall, in Acts 9:11–12, how clearly He knew all about the latest addition to His flock—where he was lodging, what he had been seeing, what he was actually doing at that very moment; and all about that other of His sheep, in Acts 10:5–6—where he was, and what he would do. Oh, yes, He has intimate acquaintance with all His sheep, with you and me.

And so *(b) The shepherd chooses the path accordingly*—He will lead them along no road too rough or stony for their feet; He "will not suffer you to be tempted above that ye are able" (1 Cor. 10:13). When a friend was watching a grocer's little son helping his father move some goods from one side of the shop to the other his little arms outstretched for his father to pile on the packets, he said, "That's enough; you can't manage any more"; to which the small son indignantly replied, "Father knows how much I can carry." Yes, indeed; and with finger pointed heavenwards, we can say the same. And He will graciously adjust the burden to our shoulder, the path to our feet. How infinitely desirable, then, that He should choose our path for us, than that we should stumble along some way of our own choice.

Knowing, therefore, what the afternoon holds for the sheep (c) *The shepherd bids them gather quietly round Himself for a while* before going on. It is ever so; and the journey and the task are always the better done for the halt that has prepared the strength for them. At God's behest, Moses tells the children of Israel in Exodus 14:15 that they are to "Go forward"—a command that made tremendous tax upon their faith and energy. But, before they moved, they were, in verse 13, told first to "Stand still"—a halt of greatest significance for the subsequent fulfillment of the mighty adventure. Elijah, too, can teach us the same lesson. In 1 Kings 18:1 he is told, "Shew thyself"—which involved the great clash with Ahab, and the mighty opposition of the whole body of the idolatrous priesthood; but he is told first, in 1 Kings 17:3 "Hide thyself"—during which time, at Cherith, and at Zarephath, he learned many things that were to fit him for the tremendous struggle that lay ahead. God's order and plan ever is Cherith before Carmel. Did not Paul go "into Arabia" (Gal. 1:17) before emerging upon his apostolic ministry? Why "even the youths shall faint and be weary, and the young men shall utterly fall: but they that wait upon the LORD shall renew their strength; they shall mount up with wings as eagles; they shall run and not be weary; and they shall walk, and not faint" (Isa. 40:30–31). Mounting, running, walking are preceded by the all-important waiting. Think of the band of the Master's disciples after the resurrection, and on the eve of the ascension, eager to be off on the glorious commission to proclaim the Gospel far and wide, almost chafing at the strange delay; "but wait," He had said (Acts 1:4). Yes, waiting before working is the rule: and that ten days' halt was a great preparation for the coming to them of the Holy Spirit, in whose might and wisdom they could then go forth to serve aright.

So from all angles—relaxation, recuperation, rehabilitation —we thank God for the noon-tide halt: the sheep will fare all the better for the pause. There is a wonderful marginal reading in Joel 3:16, which may profitably close this chapter. The text says, "The LORD will be the hope of His people," but the margin has "harbor" for "hope"—the harbor of His people: what a beautiful figure! Why does the ship run into harbor? For rest, for repair and for recommissioning: the very things that we have been considering throughout the chapter. He will not only *give* these things, but *be* these things to all His trusting and obedient people. What a Shepherd we have!

Chapter Four

THE AFTERNOON PROGRESS

"He leadeth me in the paths of righteousness for his name's sake."

The rays of the sun have now cooled down a bit, and once more life in the flock is astir, and preparations for the progress are afoot.

THE SHEEP GOES ON

There has been a need and a call for rest, but that is not the main business of a sheep's life—nor of ours. The Christian life is not a glorious lie-down, nor sit-down, though if you watched some Christians you might suppose that it was. They need very badly the searching word of Joshua to Israel, "How long are ye slack to go to possess the land?" (Josh. 18:3).

"Paths" is a symbol, not of rest, but of progress. *(a) That halt was meant to prepare for the paths*—to get the sheep ready to face again the dust, and heat, and problems of the way. What a glorious time the Intimate Three had with the Master up on the Transfiguration Mount. Peter was for staying there. He said, "Let us make three tabernacles" (Mark 9:5); but the Mount was not granted for that. The Vision, the Voice were given for the Valley where were an afflicted boy and a distracted father, and a critical enemy, and an eager multitude. The story is told of a monk, who, on a certain occasion, became very conscious of the Master's presence in his cell. His heart was filled with rapture and adoring worship at the vision of Him that was there vouchsafed. Alas, the bliss was broken into by the sounding of a bell, that called him to some duty—which, in his ecstasy, he was minded to neglect. However, his vow of obedience prevailed; and, though with sad regret, he went to perform his task. On returning later, he found, to his uttermost joy, that the Presence and the Vision were still there, and the Master greeted his return by saying, "If thou had'st stayed, I had gone." Be it ever noted that, on all counts, the vision is to be the prelude of the venture and the victory.

So we see further illustration of the fact that *(b) Those paths are meant to picture what the Christian life is to be like*—a constant progress. What would you think of a sheep who persistently sat down and refused to go on? And what will you think of a Christian who acts very much in the same manner? You must have noticed in your studies of the New Testament how frequently the notion of progress comes into the figures employed to depict the believer's life. Over and over again it is called a "walk," as in Colossians 2:6; or a "run" as in Hebrews 12:1; or a "step" as in 1 Peter 2:21; or a "path," as here in Psalm 23:3; or even as "the Way," as in Acts 9:2. We are not meant to be today where we were yesterday, but always further on. Even if there is nothing noteworthy to record, or even if there are difficulties and dangers to be surmounted, still we are intended to carry on. When Christopher Columbus was on his voyage which ended in the discovery of America, the log-book of his ship contained entries of exciting events of both good or evil omen; but day after day there was nothing to record, and so page after page of that sea diary contained the same, almost monotonous sentence, "Today we sailed on!" Over and over and over again it was the same; nothing happened—except the best thing that could have happened: they sailed on. What fixed purpose and firm pertinacity are in the words. Something very like it is to be seen in Hebrews 6:1, "Let us go on." We are to leave the foundation principles (not to leave them behind us, but to leave them beneath us) and to go on from one stage of perfection, to the next, and the next, until we reach the final perfection in Glory. We are growing all the while, advancing all the time, and verily "the path of the just is as the shining light, that shineth more and more unto the perfect day" (Prov. 4:18). So the sheep goes on. But notice, next, that—

THE SHEEP GOES AFTER

We are back, you see, at the thing that we emphasized in an earlier chapter— "He leadeth me." How favorite a word it is of the Master's, that word "Follow." It is not His first word to men: that is "Come," and only when, as repentant sinners, we leave our sin and turn to trust Him as our Savior has He any other word for us. His first word to believers is "Follow." From Matthew's Gospel (4:18–19) you might suppose that, at their first interview with the Lord Jesus, Peter and Andrew were bidden to follow; but we know from John's record (1:37–42) that they had had a previous introduction when He said "Come." I have no doubt that is a clue, and that the same rule pertained in the cases of James and John, and of Matthew, and of others. Incidentally, I think His third word was "Go." First, "Go *home* . . . and tell them" (Mark 5:19); next, "Go out . . . into the streets and lanes . . . into the highways and hedges" (Luke 14:21–23), that is, into your *neighborhood*; then "Go ye into

41

all the *world*" (Mark 16:15). Yes; but first "come" yourself, and then "follow" Him. We never forget that 1 Peter 2:21 speaks of "Christ . . . leaving us an example, that ye should follow His steps."

May I point out that the Hebrew word translated here as *"leadeth"* is not the same word as is rendered likewise in verse 2? The Revised Version marks the distinction by giving us *"guideth"* in this verse 3. There is a real difference between the two. In the first case what is implied is just that He goes in front; but in the second, that He has to give the direction. For mark, please, that it is not "roads" we are dealing with, but "paths," only mountain tracks: not easy to find and when found, not easy to keep. The eastern shepherd is expert at picking out these almost hidden tracks; just as our Good Shepherd is so able to pick out our way for us through all the perplexities of life, if only we will follow.

When we spoke earlier of His leadership we enumerated several of the ways in which He makes known His way; but now the situation has become more difficult, His will is not so easy to see. We reiterate those earlier secrets, adding one or two others, which He often offers as means whereby the guidance may be detected: Scripture, and conscience, and example, and advice, and circumstance—and sometimes by a direct voice; only, in this last case, we must be careful to test it by the Word, for He will never guide us into anything that conflicts with Scripture.

One condition is essential, and fundamental, to our ever enjoying His guidance, and that is a perfect willingness to do His will if only He will make plain what His will is. As John 7:17, has it, "If any man will do His will, he shall know . . ." How He will make it clear we must not dictate; but we may feel that it is His responsibility to do so—and our responsibility just to follow. Sometimes we seek to know His will about a matter, or a course of action, but with the proviso, at the back of our mind, that, if it falls in with what we want, we will certainly do it. We are not prepared to undertake to do it until we know what it is. "Let not that man think that he shall receive anything of the Lord," says James 1:7, in speaking of this very subject of guidance under the guise of "wisdom." The rule of the road for the Christian is 2 Corinthians 5:17, "We walk by faith, not by sight," part of the meaning of which is surely that, if we would know which road we are to take, we must be prepared to take it before we see it! We are thus committed beforehand to take it; He is—I speak in all reverence—committed to show it. Not always, indeed, not often, far ahead, but generally a step at a time.

> *I do not ask to see*
> *The distant scene,*
> *One step enough for me.*

It is thus, step by step, that a shepherd will safely guide his sheep along the often precipitous and perilous pathways of the mountainside.

Every argument of sense and safety will urge the sheep, in its following the shepherd, to keep up close; to allow any distance between is to court disaster. So discovered Peter, who "followed . . . afar off" (Matt. 26:58), for soon he found himself over the precipice of denial, the very spot which, he had so vehemently averred, would never trap him. Let every Christian, even the most earnest, ever be on his guard, lest the evil one shall induce him to drop even ever so little behind. Satan has many "nets" for the believer's unwary feet: *(a) Popularity*—all to the good, if used for God; but so often the cause of our doing wrong, or not doing right, for fear we shall lose caste with our fellows. *(b) Pride*—even spiritual pride, if we are being blessed to others, or if we think we are making strides in the Christian life. *(c) Possessions*—there is nothing wrong in being rich, many of God's greatest servants have been so—but "the love of money [not money itself] is the root of all evil" (1 Tim. 6:10). We have seen that work in several Christians. *(d) Pleasure*—let us not fall into the opposite snare of supposing that a Christian must avoid all pleasure. Indeed not, but remember pleasure has led many astray. Perhaps the safe rules may be the right kind, the right place, the right time, the right proportion. *(e) Personal consideration*—love of self, love of ease, love of sin. Such are some of the things that have so often come between a believer and his Lord—a gap gradually widening until, while there is still a following, it is a following afar off. We must carefully and prayerfully beware of the devil's nets, and must habitually adopt the attitude of Psalm 25:15, "Mine eyes are ever toward the LORD; for he shall pluck my feet out of the net"—eyes off the "net," the temptation; eyes off the "feet," the self; eyes on the Lord, the deliverer. "Eyes right" is a command of exceeding importance for Christian soldiers. Remember "when the woman saw" (Gen. 3:6); and Achan's "when I saw" (Josh. 7:21); and Peter's "when he saw" (Matt. 14:30). Oh, for grace to avoid every inducement to loiter by the way and to lag behind the Shepherd, who is ever on ahead. The old chorus still avails, "Keep close to Jesus all the way." And so we come to our next main consideration.

THE SHEEP GOES RIGHT

"Paths of righteousness" simply means right paths; and the sheep is utterly dependent on its shepherd, for it cannot find the right paths for itself. But the shepherd knows the ground, the hidden tracks, the safe places, the pitfalls, the danger spots, and if the sheep goes close after him, it will go right. The application for ourselves is plain. "All the paths of the LORD are mercy and truth" (Ps. 25:10). His path for us is right. *(a) It may not always seem right*. It must have appeared all wrong to Israel when, in Exodus 13:17, "God led them not through the way . . . of the Philistines, although that was near." Short cuts often prove the longest way round. As a matter of fact, He "guided them in the wilderness like a flock" (Ps. 78:52), whether they understood the way, or even approved the way, or not. Have you sometimes, from the summit of a mountain, looked back on the road by which you climbed? So will it be when we get "up yonder." We shall look back on life, and wonder at the way we came. The route will all be explained then: those rough places that we resented, those dark places that we dreaded, those tedious places that we hated. How different they will all look in retrospect, from up there, and how eternally grateful we shall be that we had such a Shepherd to guide us right.

Mark, then, that *(b) It would not be right if he failed us in this.* What sort of a reputation would a shepherd get if he were constantly leading his flock wrong? Truly, he would get a very bad name. So David here knows that the path will be right "for His Name's sake," even if for no other reason. His very name of Shepherd demands that He shall lead the sheep in right paths. Dr. Davidson says, "God does many things for His Name's sake, that He may be true to His own character, for He cannot deny Himself." And this is always a prevailing plea in His ear. Do you recall how, when, for the sin of the golden calf, God said He would destroy the people, Moses urged that they might be spared, on the ground of what might be thought and said about Him? "Wherefore should the Egyptians speak, and say, For mischief did he bring them out, to slay them?" (Exod. 32:12). And how jealous, and zealous, was Joshua for the honor of God's Name! Think of him, on his face before God, after the sorry defeat at Ai, not knowing why it was, nor what to do. There, in Joshua 7:9, we listen to him. "The Canaanites . . . shall hear of it . . . and cut off our name from the earth." Our name gone, nevermore to be remembered among the sons of men—that, indeed, would be bad enough;

but worse, far worse is this, "What wilt thou do unto thy great name?" Other things had their own particular importance; but, for Joshua, nothing in all the world was of such great moment as the high honor of His name. And we so glibly speak it, so carelessly write it! Do you know that, when copying the Scriptures, the Jewish scribes never wrote the divine name without first cleansing their pens, or taking up new ones, and, indeed, never did trust themselves to write the one name, Jehovah, but always substituted another in its place? Superstition, did you say? Yes, perhaps so; but I am bound to confess that, for my own part, for many years now, I have liked to pen the name of God in capital letters. It can help in giving an increased feeling of reverence.

I fancy we Christians need to learn how to use His name *(a)* as *the protection from harm*, "The name of the LORD is a strong tower" (Prov. 18:10); *(b)* as *the plea in prayer*, "whatsoever ye shall ask in my name" (John 14:13); *(c)* as *the power against evil*, "In the name of Jesus Christ . . . rise up and walk" (Acts 3:6); *(d) as the police of thoughts*, "bringing into captivity every thought to the obedience of Christ" (2 Cor. 10:5), arresting in the name of the King every wandering thought, for example, in prayer, every evil thought that forces an entrance into the mind. I think some of us are only just beginning to realize the power of the name when properly used. You see, God sets great store by His name; and the very fact that any wrong leading of the sheep would tarnish that name in the mind of men is sufficient guarantee, even if there were no other, that He will choose the "right path" for us.

Of course, *(c) It cannot be proved right if we do not follow it.* If the sheep were a sentient animal (as, certainly, we are), it would be perfectly possible to hold theoretically the opinion that the shepherd's paths were accurately chosen and yet to have no personal, practical experience of how right they were. I am afraid there are so many scriptural truths of which we

46

have theoretical, but no experimental, knowledge. As we sheep follow closely in His wake we shall prove for ourselves how wonderful is His power to lead, and to keep. An old-time peculiar preacher used to tell of an imaginary conversation between two members of a flock. Starting out one morning, a silly, delicate little sheep bleated its unworthy and unreasonable fears. "Oh, dear," it said in the Baa-Baa dialect, which of course, only very peculiar preachers understand, "I am sure I shall not be able to keep the shepherd." To which its experienced and robust sheep-mate replied, "You stupid thing, it's not your business to keep the shepherd, it's the shepherd's business to keep you." Its own business was simply to keep up! Ah, thank God, He who is "able to save" (Heb. 7:25) is also "able to keep" (Jude 24), and, indeed, "able to do exceeding abundantly above all that we ask or think [of asking]" (Eph. 3:20). This is the kind of Shepherd that we arc called to follow, and as we keep near to Him we shall, for ourselves, appreciate how "right" His paths are. And moreover, we shall come to realize that in Him we have, not merely a guide-post, which says, "*That* is the way," but a guide, who says, "*This* is the way, walk ye in it" (Isa. 30:21); so much so, in fact, that He actually declares, not simply, "I shew the Way," but "I am the Way" (John 14:6). If, in Palestine, you were not sure of your road, shall we say, to Bethlehem, and overtook a fellow-traveler and asked him the way, if he were going in the same direction he would say, "I am the Way," implying an invitation to join up with him who knew the way and travel together. So does the Good Shepherd offer Himself to His sheep as the Way, in Person, and His company—as we shall emphasize presently—to journey with them, but always, as in Mark 10:32, "before them . . . as they followed."

One last thought about that path. *(d) It will not be right just for ourselves alone.* In 1 Thessalonians 1:6, Paul makes the claim, "Ye became followers of us and of the LORD," suggesting that so closely was he following that any who followed him would *ipso facto* be following Christ. I wonder how many of us would dare to make the same claim? There is no question that such is the weight and lure of personal influence that many do, for good or ill, follow their fellows. How important it is, therefore, that we should make sure that we ourselves are walking in the right way. There is an interesting word in Hebrews 12:13, which runs, "Make straight paths for your feet, lest that which is lame be turned out of the way"—not, you notice, for your own sake merely, but for the sake of the weaker ones, the younger ones, who may be following up behind.

A certain accomplished climber took his wife and little boy with him to Switzerland to give them the holiday, not that they should do any mountaineering. One day the little fellow heard his father making plans for a big climb to start very early the next morning, and, although he was quite well aware that it was against orders the adventurous small person decided that, all unbeknown to his father, he would go too. Sure enough, in the darkness the next morning he, like his father, dressed and at a safe distance started out from the hotel. All unsuspecting what was happening behind him, father reached the base of his mountain and began the ascent—quite easy at the first, and presently a bit more hazardous for a novice but still quite safe for one experienced like himself. Then, all of a sudden, he heard something that almost made his heart stop beating and his blood run cold—the voice of his wee son, "Look out, Daddy, I'm coming." What he was now doing was all right for him, but full of peril for the child—and the child was following him. All desire for further climbing that day was taken out of him by the dizzy thought of the tragedy that might have been. But, tell me, are there any—younger, weaker— whom we are imperiling by going there, doing that which is all right, perhaps, for you, but a danger to those others? How anxious Paul was to do nothing which, however right in itself, would be likely to do harm to a "weaker brother." Indeed, how insistent was the Savior Himself that we put no "stumbling-block" in another's way. Sheep are such imitative creatures that where one goes, the next is sure to follow, even though it be into danger. What responsibility does that first one bear! But we too may be followed; and if we ourselves are walking closely in the Shepherd's right paths we shall automatically be making straight paths for those others. So through the afternoon we go. It is a fine motto for any Christian life: Keep on keeping on.

Chapter Five

THE EVENING SHADOW

"Yea, though I walk through the valley of the shadow of death, I will fear no evil: for thou art with me; thy rod and thy staff they comfort me."

The sheep's day is now wearing on to its close. Since that midday rest, it has been passing through all sorts of experiences not here mentioned; but in this verse it has come to a point where it enters into a time of darkness. I would have you notice that word *though*, for it seems to suggest that the dark period is only a possibility, or perchance a probability, but by no means a certainty. The psalmist does not say "when," as if it were bound to come, but "though," as if it might. But isn't death a certainty? Isn't the one thing certain in life that we shall die? My own heart flies to 1 Thessalonians 4:13 ff., where it is shown that some will not have to pass through this valley. There is coming a specific moment in history when our Lord Jesus will return, and in connection with that mighty event, those that "sleep"—all true believers who have died—will be raised, and those that are then "alive" will be changed and "caught up" without dying: no death-bed, no coffin, no funeral, no grave, no tombstone, no epitaph. We do not know the date of His coming, but we do know the fact; and if it should take place while we are still alive—it may not, but it might —then we should journey to heaven on the grave by-pass. But if that is not to be our experience, "though" we have to go the normal way, there is every blessed provision made for us. As a matter of fact, we shall see later that this "valley" is not to be conceived as referring exclusively to death only, although, of course, it includes that, but to every dark experience through which the believer may be called to pass. Again we stress that "though," for dark times do not come to all. God has His different "days," for His different purposes, for His different children. His "all-over" plan seems to be to fit His children for service hereafter, and whether down here we suffer or not appears to be determined by the kind of ministry we shall be called to exercise then. Suffering is not meaningless or purposeless. If accepted as from His loving hand, it will do something for us even now; but, above all, it will be His way of getting us ready for some service hereafter which as yet we do not see, but for which all that happens here is preparing us. So, be it for us "shadow" or sunshine, let us receive it as in His wondrous plan for us. But it is time we followed the sheep to—

THE PLACE

"The valley of the shadow." The shepherd would not dream of leading his flock down there in the daytime, for then it would be wrapped in stifling heat; but now, in the cool of the evening, the deep valley overcast by great towering, overspreading rocks and foliage, the journey is possible. For all that, it is a fearsome place for the sheep; and we can well imagine how naturally and instinctively they would shrink from it. Yet David, the experienced shepherd, would tell you that in almost all cases the sheep would face it quite calmly, so long as they knew that the shepherd was there—so implicitly do they trust their guardian and their guide and so definitely do they pass on the lesson to us. The land of Judea is pierced in every direction by these deep and narrow glens; and so, too, is life at large so rife with their dark counterparts.

But, what is this "valley" intended to stand for? As we have already suggested, not for death only, but for any time and place of dread and dark experience. Note that the Revised Version margin gives the rendering "the valley of deep darkness"; and Dr. Moffatt translates it "the glen of gloom." How many varied forms it may take! (a) *Sorrow*—few are altogether spared it, and for many it is an altogether devastating experience to have a loved-one snatched from one's side. It is not wrong to sorrow—though, thank God, if we are believers we "sorrow not, even as others which have no hope" (1 Thess. 4:13). The Master Himself was a "man of sorrows, and acquainted with grief," as, hundreds of years before, Isaiah 53:3 said He would be. (b) *Pain*—what a problem it presents to many, though so often more of a problem to those who watch over the patient than to the sufferer himself. Certainly it is one of those perplexing things about which, as John 13:7 states, "Thou knowest not now; but thou shalt know hereafter." (c) *Fear*—I believe that, if the truth were known, we should find that more people were bound by fear than we have had any idea of: fear of others, fear of circumstances, fear of illness, fear of the future, and so on. How dark a shadow it casts over many lives; but, thank God, there is a cure. (d) *Misunderstanding*—this can become a real blanket of darkness to the mind when whatever we do is misrepresented, and whatever we say is misconstrued. Any who suffer thus must be very specially on their guard lest they allow themselves to sink into a condition of self-pity. Anyhow, it is a comfort to know there is One who understands—and undertakes. (e) *Loneliness*—what a lot of these sad folks there are in the world, "one-room" people, with no one to care for them except One who "careth for you" (1 Peter 5:7); with no one to pray for them except One who "ever liveth to make intercession for them" (Heb. 7:25); with no one to stay with them except One who "will never leave thee nor forsake thee" (Heb. 13:5). Some, indeed, are forever in a crowd, yet are forever lonely in heart. *(f) Frustration*—the bane of many lives; they set out with such high hopes, but nothing has seemed to go right, nothing to "come off"; and now they are left with a sad sense of failure, and live under a gloomy cloud of depression. And so we might go on as we used to sing in our children's "candle" hymn—

> *Many kinds of darkness*
> *In this world abound.*

You see, Christians are not excused the hard places of life. Their trouble is often increased when they seek for some easier path. John Bunyan has put that plainly for us in his immortal allegory of *The Pilgrim's Progress,* when, at one stage, Christian and his fellow-pilgrim, hoping to discover an easier path, hopped over the stile into By-path Meadow—only to find what a blunder they had made.

We say again that the hard places, the dark places, are to be accepted as part of the training for the service on the other side and also for what they can do for us even in this life. I expect you remember that the late great American President, Franklin D. Roosevelt, suffered from a great physical disability. I recently came across a very interesting mention of this, in Frances Perkins' fine book *The Roosevelt I Knew,* in which she speaks of knowing him "from his somewhat arrogant youth, during the years of illness in which he underwent a spiritual transformation, and from which he emerged completely warm-hearted, with humility of spirit, and with a deeper philosophy." He came out, you see, not embittered, but enriched by his suffering, and trained for finer service to his fellow-men in the great strategic terms of his high office and for any service awaiting him yonder. Such, then, is the place to which the sheep of this psalm are led: what, so far as this shepherd observed it, was their reaction? What, I ask, is ours if, and when, we enter "the valley of Deep Darkness"? Take a lesson here, and, with wonder, mark—

THE PEACE

You cannot help noticing that, in spite of all the threat of the place, there is about this animal a strangely unexpected atmosphere of quiet. *(a) There is peace in its inward heart*—"I will fear no evil," he says; and if you could test his heart, you would find no vestige of flutter or fluster—all is calm within. Have you ever observed the contrast between Psalm 56:3, and Isaiah 12:2? The first is a very remarkable statement, and it contains a most admirable piece of advice: "What time I am afraid, I will trust in Thee." An excellent thing to do: in spite of his fears, he will do the duty, trusting God to see him through, even though he trembles the while. Two soldiers were going into battle—one, an old veteran who did not turn a hair; the other, a raw youngster shaking with fright. The older man started to jeer at his comrade for his fear, but the youngster could only reply, "Well, if you were as afraid as I am, you would turn back and run away; but I'm going to stick it out." What a magnificent answer! That was true courage; the other's, merely callousness! There was plenty of the former in many a bombed city in the air-raids of the War: many a hidden act of sublime heroism was done by unnoticed civilians—unknown, unheralded, undecorated; men, yes, and women, who shook but never shirked. It is, I say, a great thing, when we are afraid, to put our trust in God and do the thing that terrifies us—to take that stand, to say that word, to face that threat, to risk that peril.

But I mentioned a second text by way of contrast: Isaiah says, "I will trust and not *be* afraid"—a claim more remarkable still. As the Honorary Chaplain to our Beckenham Hospital it has been my privilege to stand by the bedside of many a patient, both during the War and at other times, who was about to go down into the dark valley of the Operating Theater; and while some have faced it with sheer callousness, and others in unrelieved cowardice, I have had those who have braved the dread experience with a wonderful sense of peace. How often have I given to real Christians in that hour the Lord's word in Isaiah 41:13, "I, the LORD thy God, will hold thy right hand, saying unto thee, Fear not," and not a few have testified that as they went down resting back on that pillow, so their first thought on coming-to after the anesthetic has been the remembrance of that same pillow underneath them. Some have trusted when they were afraid; others have trusted and not been afraid.

But look again at this sheep in the "valley." *(b) There is peace in its outward demeanor*—"I walk through . . ." unhurried; undisturbed! I should not have been surprised if it had had to be dragged through, if not drugged through. I should almost have expected that it would, anyhow, have trotted through or even run through; but, lo and behold, I find it quietly walking through! You see it was peaceful at heart, and therefore peaceful at large. So often it is just the opposite with us: our impulsive acts so often betray the storm and unrest within. The world is, alas, a very troubled and restless place; and I believe it gives great and even yearning heed to any who show in their outer behavior the evidence of peace in their inner being. To walk through this world, especially the difficult places, with peace on our faces and calm in our bearing is, I believe, both a great testimony to the keeping power of God and also a great influence for God on the lives of those around us. When they behold our peace, I fancy they will want to know its secret. Paul enlarges on that secret in Philippians 4:6–7, "Be careful for nothing; but in everything by prayer and supplication with thanksgiving let your requests be made known unto God. And the peace of God, which passeth all understanding, shall keep your hearts and minds through Christ Jesus." That's it: careful for nothing, prayerful for everything, thankful for anything. Then comes peace, not such as we can all understand, dependent on circumstances being all right; but such as "passeth all understanding" because it is quite independent of whatever circumstances may be like. Peace inward; and so outward.

But note once again this sheep in the "valley." (c) *There is peace in its forward look*—"I will walk *through*." The glen of gloom is no blind alley, no cul-de-sac, no terminus. There is an exit as well as an entrance, and this sheep knows that however dark, however long, it will eventually get "through." It is good for us all to remember that tunnels do not last for ever; they may be as short as a mere roadbridge, or as long as a Severn, or even a Simplon, but they all come to end. And while we are passing through we are still journeying on to our destination and we are still on the rails—those twin metals, trust and obey, which carry the gospel train safely to its terminus. It is unfortunate that when some people run into a tunnel they immediately go off the rails! That is, when trouble comes—some pain, or grief, or loss—they begin to doubt God. Why should God allow this? Why should this happen to me? I shall throw up all my religion. And so on. Oh, so sad! Whatever tunnel we come to as we travel Heavenwards, let us never lose touch and grip of the rails; let us keep to the two rails; let us trust and obey. For "heaviness may endure for a night, but joy cometh in the morning." The sheep knows that its shepherd will lead it not only into but "through" the dark valley—hence it has forward peace, as well as inward and outward peace. Ah, but all this peace does not come by chance:

there is an explanation. You have, of course, in your Bible study, learned never to neglect the little words, often of seeming insignificance but often of strategic importance in the sentence. Even so the little word "for" here. It turns out, on reflection, to be the very pivot of the whole verse. Two amazing statements are made, and "for" is the connecting link—turning the second into the reason for the first. And that brings us on now, brings the sheep on, to contemplate—

THE PRESENCE

"Thou art with me." He has not ceased to lead because it has come to a valley. Do you recall the valley after the Transfiguration mount? In Mark 9:9 it says, "They came down." Who did? Why, Peter and James and John, of course; but is that all? *Behind them*—all the glories of the mountaintop experience. *Before them*—all the problems and perplexities of the valley life: what a "come down"! Yes, but note. *Beside them*—was the Lord Jesus. He did not leave them to face the valley alone. He never does. And in His presence is the peace and power and pleasure (Ps. 16:11) that we need. One day I got into a compartment of a railway train and found at the other end of the carriage a mother and her little girl. Presently we ran into the rather long Penge tunnel, and, as it happened, there were no lights put on. As we passed into the darkness, I heard a rather cheerful voice say, "Are you there, Mummie?" But the tunnel continued; and after a bit I heard the same little voice, although this time somewhat wistful, "Are you still there, Mummie?" It was long, and dark, and noisy, and smelly, but so long as Mother was there the girl was reassured; and at last, sure enough, we ran out into the sunlight again. Someone has said

> *I'd rather walk in the dark with Him,*
> *Than travel alone in the light.*

Let us get down to it, then, and see what His presence means and implies. (1) *The Shepherd's Crook*—"Thy staff": a good, strong implement, generally with a curved head-piece. A shepherd would never travel without it. If a sheep were acting carelessly in the way, a gentle touch would remind it to be sure to keep in the right path; if a sheep had wandered out of the way and got into difficulties, hanging perilously, perhaps, in some bushes over the side of a precipice, the curved end of the crook would be such a help in the rescue. What a "comfort" to the flock was the recollection that the shepherd had his crook with him. It would, indeed, serve many purposes—for testing the firmness of the ground in front lest he lead his flock into a bog or quagmire; for use as a kind of vaulting pole when crossing a stream; for a prop, leaning his weight on which he would sometimes go to sleep, or say his prayers. Do you think there is any connection between this last and Hebrews 11:21, where we find old Jacob blessing his grandsons, and worshiping God, "leaning upon the top of his staff"? Was he, as head of the clan, acting as the shepherd of the family? Through many centuries our Bishops, acting as shepherds of a flock, have carried their pastoral staffs, or crooks.

But what is that other implement, hanging down by the man's side? (2) *The Shepherd's Club*—"Thy rod": a truly formidable weapon, made of oak, with a bulbous head, often studded with iron nails. If the staff represented the gentle tenderness of the shepherd, the rod was a symbol of his strong authority and power. This iron-studded rod is used in this sense in those words thrice found in Revelation (2:27, and 12:5, and 19:15) about ruling "with a rod of iron"; and, strange to say, it has since developed into such symbols of authority as the king's sceptre, the mayor's mace, the field marshal's baton, and even, perhaps, the churchwarden's wand. In the Old Testament, the shepherd is essentially a ruler: the King, for instance, was the shepherd of his people. The false shepherds of

Ezekiel 34 were, of course, the false rulers of Israel. The late Dr. A. J. Schofield, in his *With Christ in Palestine*, makes the interesting point that whereas normally, "every shepherd is an abomination unto the Egyptians" (Gen. 46:34), when the Hyksos, the shepherd-people, had conquered Egypt and their leaders became kings, or Pharaohs, Jacob could safely and usefully describe his men as "shepherds" to Joseph's Pharaoh, because at that period the dynasty of the shepherd kings was on the throne. "They took this club with them on the throne, and the club has become the 'sceptre' of kings ever since. When King Edward VII (we should say, George VI) was crowned in Westminster Abbey, he was holding, to all intents and purposes, the club of the Twenty-third Psalm." Let us not forget the lesson of all this, as bringing out the sovereign rights of the Good Shepherd over His flock, as well as His tender solicitude for their constant welfare.

The club has also something to say to us about His sovereign choice. How, do you suppose, were the victims chosen for the sacrifices? Leviticus 27:32 says, "All the tithe of the flock, all that passes by under the club, the tenth is holy to Jehovah." James Neil, in his wonderful *Everyday Life in the Holy Land*, explains, "It was usual, when the tenth was being taken, to bring all the animals together . . . in a pen. They were then allowed of themselves to pass out one by one through the narrow entrance, where the shepherd stood with his club, the rounded head of which was dipped in a bowl of coloring matter. As the beasts came out—thus themselves arranging the tithe with perfect impartiality—he let the head of the club fall on every tenth, marking it with a spot of color; and those thus branded were taken for the . . . sacrifices." That would suggest to me personally something of the way in which human choice comes into harmonious relation with divine election. I speak only for myself; you may find in it no such solution. Ezekiel 20:34–38 refers this practice to God's eventual dealings with

the Jewish nation: "I will cause you to pass under the club."
Dr. Gaebelein adds, "In the wilderness of people, their disper-
sion among all the nations of the world, He will plead with
them, and bring them under the rod"—not there, it would
seem, the rod of chastisement, but the rod of choice.

The sacrificial sheep are thus seen to be "marked" animals;
and they are a picture of His sheep, partakers of the death of
His Son, "crucified with Christ" (Gal. 2:20), who also have
been marked. "On your believing [see Greek] ye were sealed
with that Holy Spirit of promise" (Eph. 1:13). It is of this that
Hugh Stowell sang concerning His flock—

> *Then on each He setteth*
> *His own secret sign;*
> *They that have My Spirit,*
> *These, saith He, are Mine.*

May we "sealed" ones never "grieve" (Eph. 4:30) nor disap-
point our Shepherd. There is one other purpose of the club,
and that is, to deal with the marauding attacks of beasts and
Bedouin; but that we must leave to be dealt with in our next
chapter. Let it just now only be reiterated, "Thy rod and thy
staff they comfort me"—what a comfort they are! The
Shepherd's Crook and the Shepherd's Club, how they minister
to the peace of the flock!

And just one thing more: (3) *The Shepherd's Company*—
"Thou art with me." That, first and last; we began with it, and
we end with it. A strange thing occurred at one of the great
Keswick Convention meetings. We were singing, to lovely
Crimond of course, the hymn, "The Lord's my Shepherd."
When we came to this verse:

> *Yea, though I walk through death's dark vale,*
> *Yet will I fear none ill,*
> *For Thou art with me, and Thy rod*
> *And staff me comfort still.*

61

What *do* you think happened? Mr. Georgehan, always so helpful at the piano, made (if he will forgive me) his one mistake of the week—he left us to sing it unaccompanied, and right well it sounded! But, *unaccompanied*—that of all verses! No; we don't "walk through" that dark valley unaccompanied "for thou art with me."

Do you notice a very remarkable, and very beautiful, change in the pronoun in this fourth verse? Up till now, it has been, "He . . . He . . . He . . . He"; for the rest it is "Thou . . . Thou . . . Thou." Why that change? Simply that the psalmist has come into greater intimacy with Him; and, mark it well, that closer intimacy was begotten in the dark valley! Beloved Samuel Rutherford said, "The need and the usefulness of Christ is seen best in trials," and who should know that better than that saint of God? Surely the dark place is to be welcomed if it brings us into nearer touch, deeper communion, with God. That is why the writer of Psalm 119:71 said, "It is good for me that I have been afflicted"; and many another sufferer has borne the same testimony. The sick of the palsy would, I think, have joined this happy chorus. All those years he had been so sadly paralyzed; but it was his very sickness that brought him to his Savior and sent him home with the knowledge of "sins . . . forgiven" (Mark 2:5). I believe he would have gone back a happy man, even if his poor body had never been healed. Anyhow, I imagine that he would sometimes say, "How I thank God that I was paralyzed"; for it caused him to come to know Christ. My own beloved Mother, who, for thirty-four years, was a bed-ridden sufferer, used to say that if it had not been for her affliction she would never have known God. His Presence in the valley: how sweet it is; what peace it brings! A multitude has proved that by blessed experience.

How did Enoch walk safe in the midst of the dark valley of his time? Jude 15 will give you a hint of what he had to put up with. His secret was (Gen. 5:24) that he "walked *with God.*"

And Noah? What a depraved state was the world of his day in, how dark his time; yet he walked aright. However did he manage it? He "walked *with God*" (Gen. 6:9). How did the three young men of Daniel 3 walk unscathed and unafraid in the awful dread of their furnace of fire? It was (v. 25) the form of the "fourth" Man, walking with them. How did the Daniel of Chapter 6 come unhurt through his den of lions? It was (v. 22) the "Angel"—as I think one of the many Old Testament appearances for men of the Son of God—who walked with Him. And how shall you and I walk at peace in the dark place? Only by the same grand secret, the Presence.

If you are a Bible marker, I give you two words to sum up this glorious fourth verse. Put a neat ring around each and join the rings up. The two words are "though" and "thou."

Chapter Six

THE SUNSET HOMECOMING

"Thou preparest a table before me in the presence of mine enemies: thou anointest my head with oil; my cup runneth over."

The flock is now safely "through" the dark valley; it is not so gloomy out here; but, for all that, the evening is fast drawing in, the day's life of the sheep will soon be done. It is sunset as they come gathering home for—

THE EVENING MEAL

"Thou preparest a table before me." Before the sheep are folded for the night they must, at all hazards (and these will be considerable) have their evening sustenance provided for them. So the ever-mindful shepherd has arranged what will be needful. It was his first thought for them in their early morning; it is his last thought for them now at their close of day.

David was a king, as well as a shepherd; and many a time he would have given a great night feast to his subjects or friends.

As they came into the banqueting hall they would be anointed with the fragrant oil that was inseparably associated with festal occasions in the East, while they would find a full cup, a full table, prepared by the bountiful hospitality of their royal host. And David's vivid imagination plays with the idea that the flock sits down at just such a feast—it is all a "let's pretend," but the meal itself is real enough for the sheep: it must needs be. There is, I think, no break in the imagery of the shepherd, but only an exercise of his imagination for the sheep. "Those sheep there," he seems to say, "are just like those subjects of mine who came to my dinner last night, and their frugal meal, with its accompanying details, is in its simple way not altogether unlike what was provided for my guests in the palace."

And as we, for our part, use the imagination still further and apply the scene to the thought of the supply of our nightly sustenance, we say *(a) What a table is Holy Scripture*—for we are back again where we began, at the pasture of the Word of God, with its soul-satisfying meals. There are no restrictions in the royal dainties of this table: the "courses" are pleasant and plenty. "Thy words were found, and I did eat them; thy word was unto me the joy and rejoicing of mine heart (Jer. 15:16), "Sweeter also than honey" (Ps. 19:10). "He brought me to the banqueting house, and his banner over me was love" (Song of Sol. 2:4). As, then, we sit down to our Bible banquet, perhaps *the first course will be conviction*—some *hors d'oeuvre* of acid quality that will set the juices flowing and quicken the appetite for what is to follow; some word of truth that will convict us of our sinfulness, or of a sin. *The next course will be comfort*—as He speaks the word of forgiveness and healing, so grateful to the heart; for He never wounds but for our good. *The following course will be confidence*—for the Word of God, so utterly reliable and trustworthy, always begets trust in true believers; and there, indeed, must our confidence ever rest: not in what others say, not in what we think, not in what circumstances dictate, but in what God has declared. Let me but find a word, let me but fulfill the condition—and there let me rest. *Another course will be consistency*—for the Scriptures will ever urge upon our serious attention the words of James 1:22, "Be ye doers of the word, and not hearers only." We are to see that we live the Bible, that our conduct coincides with our creed, that in everyday practice ours may be a belief that behaves. *Maybe, a further course will be compulsion*—our study compelling us to take that action, to speak that word, that we have long known we should but have put off all this while. "Now then do it" (2 Sam. 3:18) it will say. *Often a course will be commission*—out from the inspired page will come the word that will challenge us to "Go" for our Lord hither or thither, even as it came to young Gideon (Judg. 6:14), "Go in this thy might . . . have not I sent thee?" There are few things so mighty in God's service as the sense of being sent. And after all this, assuredly, *the last course will be content*—as we close the Book, and say our "Grace" of grateful thanks for so soul-satisfying a meal as His Word provides. All this has come to us in the course of our feeding at such "green pastures."

And *(b) How wonderfully it has been prepared.* It is all so easy for our enjoyment; but what expenditure of cost lies behind it. When you have given a supper party, you know how much preparation was entailed before; in the words of Luke 14:17 you could say, "Come, for all things are now ready." Before this scripture-feast was "now ready" for you there was the inspiration of the Holy Spirit upon all who wrote; the preservation of their work; the translation, printing, dispatching and delivering of the Book for the peoples, for you and me; the pains and perils of many who suffered that we might have it in our own tongue. The cost in money, in energy, in sacrifice was very high; and here are we just simply taking up the precious volume, and most times quite oblivious of the price of the banquet to our Blessed Host. God give us ever thankful hearts, that the feast is spread, and that we are invited. You know, it was often only at great pains that the eastern shepherd was able to find suitable pasture for the evening meal of his flock. I wonder if they were grateful? I know they would be resentful, if they didn't get it!

So *(c) The table is spread* "before me," as our verse says. It is ours now, to use, or to refuse: you can lead a sheep to the pasture, but you can't make it eat. I do know that some of the Lord's sheep are very irregular about their Bible meals; and then they wonder why their spiritual vitality is so low, why they are not as strong and healthy Christians as other people or as they themselves once were. Like some poor folk, they have not had a decent meal for ages: there lies their Bible now dust-covered on the shelf, and sometimes in church they sing in William Cowper's plaintive lines:

> *Where is the blessedness I knew*
> *When first I saw the Lord?*

My friend Mr. Hudson Pope used to answer them, "I'll tell you where it is. It's up there on the shelf!" Oh, get it down, dust it, open it, study it, and neglect it nevermore. None of us, not even sheep, can grow strong or show health or know contentment without our proper food.

And what shall we say of that other table of our sustenance, the sweet Feast of Remembrance? "This do in remembrance of me," He said, (Luke 22:19); and surely they who fail to feast will fail of much enrichment of soul and much enlargement for service. Our Church of England refers to its ordained clergy as "ministers of the Word and sacraments"—allotting the Word first place, but giving the sacrament due place. And, going back to our Lord's institution of the Supper, I am bound to say that I cannot understand how any true believer can do other than obey His plain command, accept His gracious invitation, and make much of the high privilege. Being, as it is, and as it was originally intended to be, a reminder of the exceeding love of the broken body and the outpoured blood, such an occasion will surely feed our heart's devotion and our life's sacrifice. Let us regularly be found at the Memorial Supper of the Lord, until we sit down at the Marriage Supper of the Lamb (Rev. 19:9). Returning now to the flock's evening meal, we are drawn up fast by—

THE ENEMY MENACE

"In the presence of mine enemies." James Neil tells us that, at sundown, the wild beasts will come out of their dens. Sheep and shepherd will become aware of the tramp of the wild boar, the baying of the wolf, the yell of the jackal, the scream of the hyena, and, worse than all, the leopard: if he is about, all the others will fear and be still and silent. Then, too, the viper will bite the noses of the sheep as they feed. How alert and how brave the shepherd must be; how dependent on him the sheep must be. You see, as John Freeman says, "others than the sheep are . . . looking for their evening meal." That meal is partaken of by the flock in often perilous circumstances. So much will conspire to prevent their having it; but the shepherd will, by every ruse, see that they do have it. For sheer, quiet, unheralded courage commend me to these stout-hearted men. David himself, the erstwhile keeper of the flocks, knew of these perils from his own personal experience: as recorded in 1 Samuel 17:34–35 his pluck and prowess were displayed in his encounters with a lion and a bear. In such a predicament, what "comfort," both for sheep and shepherd, will be the club, the "rod" by his side.

So, too, will Satan do his diabolical utmost to stop our getting the food of the Word, for he knows that if he can do that he will succeed in starving the soul. Because he knows, if we do not, the power of the Book, he is downright afraid of people

69

reading it. Both prayer and the Scripture are anathema to him. You remember the lines in the old hymn:

> *Satan trembles when he sees*
> *The weakest saint upon his knees.*

A colporteur of the British and Foreign Bible Society was pushing his wares through the villages of Portugal, selling the books at a very low price to the peasants because of their poverty. He evidently knew that hymn just mentioned, for, on his barrow, he had this placard,

> *Satan trembles when he sees*
> *Bibles sold as cheap as these.*

The enemy menace to our meal is very real; it is only as we keep constantly looking to our Shepherd that we shall overcome these fears and threats. You have heard our foe and his henchmen described as "that old Serpent" (Rev. 12:9); "wolves" (Luke 10:3); "dogs" (Phil. 3:2); "a roaring lion, [that] walketh about, seeking whom he may devour" (1 Peter 5:8). In the Shepherd-passage of John 10:1–13 we are warned against our three kinds of enemies. There is the open enemy, the "wolf"; there is the secret enemy, the "thief"; and there is the false friend, the "hireling." From each we must be daily protected, and "the Good Shepherd" of the same passage is the very one to give us protection and deliverance. It is a very moving sight to watch the behavior of a flock of sheep browsing amid the grass when a sudden danger arises: instantly all faces are lifted and all eyes turned—not to the danger, but to the shepherd! So, too, says Psalm 25:15, is our safety found in Him. Truly, the soul's enemies are no less real than the sheep's: perhaps they are all the more venomous and dangerous by reason of the fact that they are mostly unseen. And now comes a very different part of the flock's sunset experience—

THE EASING MEDICAMENT

"Thou anointest my head with oil." Oil and wine were, of course, chief medicines of the East (Luke 10:34). (I wonder if the appreciation of this fact would give any guidance in the interpretation of James 5:14?) I have a strong feeling that David refers here to the oil of healing, rather than to the oil of feasting. After all, it calls to mind a very familiar sunset scene at the fold. In the course of the travels of the day the sheep will often get wounded by a thorn, or a bite; its head would so easily get bruised by sudden contact with a rock. And there, as the flock comes home at eventide, stands the shepherd, with his horn of oil; he will carefully scrutinize each head as it passes, and ease with his comforting medicament any that are hurt.

We, too, have *(a) Our maladies.* Have we sometimes come home at nightfall with *a shamed face?* We have been so little like we have wanted to be; we have both by commission and by omission, fallen so far short of God's plan and purpose for us; we have been so slow to seize and even to see, the opportunities that have come our way; we have been ashamed or afraid when the chance was given us, to own up to our allegiance to Christ. A traveler, talking one evening with one of the monks of the St. Bernard Hospice in Switzerland, observed one of the famous dogs as, head down and tail drooping, it slunk by them to the kennels. "Is that dog ill?" he asked. "No; it has happened to him on the mountain-side that he found no one to help, and he has come home so ashamed." No one to help—that could not have been said of us; but, perhaps, this, that we did not help those we could. No wonder we are ashamed at sunset.

Or, maybe, it is *an aching heart.* Some deep sorrow has come to us today in the loss of a dear one, or our eyes have been opened in sad disillusionment to the true character of one we had always trusted and esteemed; some shattering blow has fallen upon our pride or prospects; some verdict has been pronounced that has left us reeling. No wonder our heart is sore.

Perchance our difficulty is *a troubled mind*. The future is very disturbing; the clouds are heavy, the air threatening with thunder; it is not only ourselves we think of, but our loved ones are involved; how will they fare if the storm breaks? Anxiety and perplexity combine to vex our heart almost to snapping point.

With others it may be *a wounded spirit*. We imagined that we were quite capable of tackling that job, and our failure has proved a bitter pill; it was gall to us, though we tried to hide it, that another was advanced over our head; a feeling of unsuspected inferiority settles down on us; in our former self-esteem, we never thought it would be like this.

Or else it is *a guilty conscience*. It really was not quite straight to act as we did; the way we filled in that form was rather unscrupulous; we were not a little underhanded in our behavior; what we said was not quite a lie, but it was near enough to it, and anyhow it deliberately gave a false impression as it was meant to do.

How often the trouble has been *a black-stained soul*. We prayed this morning, "Grant that this day we fall into no sin"; but alas, through our own fault we have so fallen and, as night draws on, we feel we must not, cannot, sleep with such stains upon us, and we long for divine forgiveness and cleansing; as, in the quiet of the gathering darkness, we face Him there alone we are inclined to make no excuses, but only to crave His pardon and His peace. Such, at sunset, are some of the maladies of us His Sheep.

But we have *(b) Our remedies*. In the Bible "oil" is outstandingly a type and symbol of the Holy Spirit, and He it is who, in His varied ministries, brings healing to His sad or stricken sheep at the close of the day. Sometimes it is as *the oil of teaching*—helping the perplexed to understand; for as

1 John 2:20 says, "ye have an unction from the Holy One, and ye know all things [that ye need to know]." Sometimes it is as *the oil of joy*—bringing His gladness for our sadness; "the oil of joy for mourning" as Isaiah 61:3 says, verse 1 showing us what is backed up by Galatians 5:22, that this is part of the fruit of "the Spirit of the Lord." Sometimes it is as *the oil of power*—the very thing for those whose day has filled them with a disappointing sense of weakness and failure. He "anointed Jesus . . . with the Holy Ghost and with power" (Acts 10:38), as He does for all His trusting children. Sometimes it is as *the oil of pardon*—restoring to us our unity and fellowship with God, "like precious ointment upon the head . . ." (Ps. 133:2). Sometimes it is as *the oil of freshness*—so infinitely welcome to souls that have come home jaded and weary after the day's round: "I shall be anointed with fresh oil" (Ps. 92:10).

It would seem that for every malady there is a remedy, in one or other of the gracious ministries of the Holy Spirit. Like as Christian saw in the Interpreter's House in the *Pilgrim's Progress*, the man's fire persisted, and resisted all attempts of the water thrower to put it out, because on the other side of the wall there was a man who continually poured oil, to feed the flame and to defeat the schemes of the enemy; so whatever efforts the adversary may exert to douse or extinguish the fire within, there is at hand always the oil of God's grace to keep the flame bright, the continual gift to us of the Holy Spirit. Surely one of the best benedictions, as we arrive weary and worn each night is this refreshing and renewing experience, "Thou anointest my head with oil." Still one more blessing of the sunset hour is—

THE EXTRA MEASURE

"My cup runneth over." This is a last refreshing drink for the sheep before it settles down for the night—not, you observe, just a drop or two to moisten the mouth, but a great, long drink, that will satisfy. The "cup" is filled to the brim, and over.

How like that is to the refreshing gifts of God—always so lavish. If it is life we crave— "I am come that they might have life, and that they might have it *more abundantly*" (John 10:10). If it is peace—"*Perfect* peace, and at such a time" (Ezra 7:12). If it is victory—"In all these things we are *more than conquerors*, through him that loved us" (Rom. 8:37). If it is grace—"He giveth *more* grace" (James 4:6). If it is joy— "Believing, ye rejoice with joy *unspeakable*" (1 Peter 1:8). If it is power—"What is the *exceeding greatness* of his power to us-ward who believe" (Eph. 1:19). If it is salvation—"How shall we escape, if we neglect *so great* salvation?" (Heb. 2:3). If it is blessing—"I will pour you out a blessing that there shall *not be room enough* to receive it" (Mal. 3:10). If it is the Holy Spirit—"they were all *filled* with the Holy Spirit" (Acts 2:4). We have already, in an earlier study, quoted that extraordinary passage wherein Paul is moved to pile up the words to indicate what is the measure of His giving: "Now unto him that is able to do *exceeding abundantly above* all that we ask or think" (Eph. 3:20).

Such is the magnificence and munificence of the gifts of God. Why are our Christian lives often so poverty-stricken, when such abundant riches are ours for the asking—indeed, for the taking? We so greatly need to pray that prayer of His disciples of long ago, "Lord, increase our faith" (Luke 17:5); for faith is the soul's hand that takes what He offers; and the bigger the hand, the more it can grasp and hold. There was an old believer who, at the prayer-meeting one night, said, "Lord, I can only hold a little, but I can overflow lots." Well, his holding capacity could be mightily increased; but, in any case, that "overflow" would not be wasted—others could get that. To go back to the Malachi quotation, that part of the blessing which there was "not room enough to receive" could be passed on to others. "In him a well," says John 4:14; "out of him . . . rivers," says John 7:38.

When I was a curate at St. Matthew's, Croydon, under that grand Vicar, the Rev. W. E. Daniels, I used to visit beloved old Mrs. Codner, the hymn-writer. One day, in my youthful impudence, I ventured to criticize a word in one of her well-known compositions:

> *Lord, I hear of showers of blessing*
> *Thou art scattering full and free,*
> *Showers the thirsty land refreshing,*
> *Let some droppings fall on me.*

Such was my eloquence on the point that I convinced the old lady, and she said that I might alter the word whenever I wished. I am passing the permission on to you. Which was the word, did you say? Why, dear reader, look at the lines again! It was that word "droppings," of course. When "showers" are about, I am not going to be satisfied with "droppings"—are you? I want to enjoy to the very utmost that extra measure of blessing that He is so graciously ready to bestow, that I may join with His many other sheep in the glad testimony, "My cup runneth over." That is a fine thought for the sunset hour.

Chapter Seven

THE NIGHTFALL REFLECTION

"Surely goodness and mercy shall follow me all the days of my life; and I will dwell in the house of the LORD for ever."

The sheep's day at last is over; and as, safely in the fold, it lies down to sleep, it would, if it were a reasonable creature, have certain thoughts and reflections: three such impressions we gather as we ponder the Psalm's closing verse.

AN AIR OF CONFIDENCE

To begin with, *look at that word "surely."* That is the sheep's conclusion from all that has gone before: the past guarantees the future. Old John Newton, one-time drunken sailor and reprobate, but afterwards deeply loved poet and pastor, thinking back on the saving, sustaining, satisfying grace of God, wrote—

> *His love in time past*
> *Forbids me to think*

> *He'll leave me at last*
> *In sorrows to sink;*
> *Each sweet Ebenezer*
> *I have in review,*
> *Confirms His good promise*
> *To see me right through.*

That is the tenor of the whole psalm; indeed, of the whole Bible. If, as we saw at the end of our last study, it deals so much with superlatives of gift, it also deals so emphatically with positives of statement. There is so little in the Scriptures of the perhaps, the perchance, the possibly, or the peradventure. Dr. van Dyke has said, "Our age is an age of doubt, whose fitting crest would be an interrogation mark, and its appropriate motto 'Query.'" How true that is; and how wholly different from the Book, whose note is certainty, and whose professed object is "that ye may know" (1 John 5:13). Uncertainty is no use to sheep. It has no mind of its own, and it demands that its shepherd shall know his own mind—no "dithering," as the Scots would say. Luke's preface (1:4) could be truly written, by way of introduction, over the whole Bible—"That thou mightest know the certainty of those things wherein thou hast been instructed."

Or, *look at that word "shall."* Could anything be more clear, or more definite? This is a man who is quite persuaded that what he says will most surely come to pass. And what is that? "Goodness and mercy shall follow me"—that has been, and shall be, his glad experience. *Goodness* is God's hand that proffers the gift; *Mercy* is God's heart that prompts the hand to give. C. H. Spurgeon used to say that those two were like "guardian angels"; but I would suggest that we keep to our metaphor and look at this as a happy procession through the days and ways of life—first, the shepherd; followed by the sheep; followed by the sheep-dogs. All through the day the shepherd has been in the lead and he has been on the lookout for any enemies that might lie and lurk ahead. Only now, at the end of the day, has the sheep become conscious that it has been followed by a couple of dogs who, among other purposes, are set there to perform the office of rearguard, with a wide-awake eye for any possible enemies in the rear. I so well remember years ago a big meeting at the Queen's Hall, in London, at which the chief speaker was to be the Home Secretary, the Rt. Hon. Sir William Joynson-Hicks, afterwards Lord Brentford. As people were arriving, I happened to be standing, talking with a friend by the platform entrance, when a handsome car drove up and out got "Jix" himself, smiling and immaculate as usual. The point, however, that so greatly impressed me and stuck in my memory, was that—where they came from I don't know—he was immediately followed by, covered by, two plain-clothes detectives. It was wonderfully done, and so efficient that none of us nearby could have done the minister any harm. No less wonderful is the work of our sheep-dogs for us the sheep. The gospel of the rearguard is a very encouraging message.

We may have many enemies behind us that would do us hurt if they could. *(a)* There are what John Freeman calls "the blood-hounds of hereditary taint and constitutional defect and transmitted tendency." Thank God, the sheep-dogs are quite well able to keep them at bay; for "where sin abounded, grace did much more abound" (Rom. 5:20). *(b)* There are the memories of past sins, which may dog our footsteps, till the sheep-dogs send them scampering away; even as in Martin Luther's case, who, when, in a moment of realistic imagination, he seemed to find Satan in his room, and to hear his very voice saying, "You think yourself a very fine fellow, Martin," as he unrolled before his face a scroll of his past sins. Luther replied, "It is all true, Satan; but the blood of Jesus Christ His Son cleanseth us from all sin" (1 John 1:7)—with which remark Luther is reputed to have thrown the inkpot at the devil's head, an action quite unnecessary since the enemy was already hurrying from the room. *(c)* There may be an old sinful habit that has forged a seemingly unbreakable chain about you, whose hostile shape like some gaunt, gray wolf is ever dragging at your heels. Fortunately the sheep-dogs know how to master sin-wolves, for

> *He breaks the power of cancell'd sin,*
> *He sets the prisoner free.*

"If the Son therefore shall make you free, ye shall be free indeed" (John 8:36). Verily, we are safe against all pursuing foes, against the condemning and crippling power of our own past, because between them and us is the protection of God's goodness and mercy. Between them and us—yes, do you recall Gehazi's young successor, so frightened at the encircling force of the Syrian armies at Dothan, and Elisha's prayer for him: "LORD . . . open his eyes, that he may see" (2 Kings 6:17), how he saw that between them and their enemies was the protecting host of heaven? How well served for protection—as for all else—is the sheep of His pasture, both before and behind. As Isaiah puts it, "The LORD will go before you; and the God of Israel will be your rearward" (Isa. 52:12). How good, then, for the sheep is this air of confidence—not in our self, but in our Shepherd; knowing that as yesterday, and today, so tomorrow, "Surely . . . shall"! Which is where we move on to our next thought—

AN ASSURANCE OF CONSTANCY

"All the days of my life." Two thoughts arise. *(a) How variable will be the days*—both in quantity, and in quality. Spring days, and summer days, and autumn days, and winter days; Sundays and fun-days, week-days and weak days; days of sunshine and shadow; days of peace and peril; days of rest and rush; days of plain-sailing and perplexity. No day can be envisaged in the which the vigilance of God will be relaxed. "All the days," and all the day, He will be at hand, reverently we say it, at the sheep's beck and call.

Note, too *(b) How reliable will be the shepherd.* The sheep will wander from the right path, the "hireling" will flee in danger's hour (John 10:12–13), but the Shepherd "abideth faithful"; He is in front, and the sheep-dogs behind, and we His sheep are happily sandwiched in between. Will you remember that when days are dark, and ways are difficult? I expect you will have heard the story of how David Livingstone died. The Lord had shepherded that great missionary-explorer "all the days of his life," through days of daring, and disappointment, and disease, and delight; and now it was night-fall. And early in the morning they found him, kneeling at his bed-side, but his spirit had gone to "dwell in the house of the LORD for ever." On the bed was his little pocket Bible, lying open at the last page of Matthew's gospel; and in the margin, alongside one of the verses, were the words, in Livingstone's handwriting, "The word of a Gentleman." It was at verse 20, "Lo, I am with you alway"—"all the days"!

Ah, yes, "surely"—how reliable He is, and His "goodness and mercy"! The Revised Version margin has "only" for that "surely," which former Dr. Davidson considers the better translation of the word David used. The psalmist, by its employment, affirms that what follows us all the days of our life will be "only goodness and mercy"—nothing else will be allowed; so that we may know that all which is allowed to come is—though we may not always recognize it as such, of that quality. We do not forget that this "goodness" not only "follows" to protect us, but also sometimes to pursue us as, for one cause or another, we run away from God. This, you remember, is the theme of Francis Thompson's remarkable autobiographical poem, "The Hound of Heaven." With what zeal and loving energy the sheep-dog sought to catch the wandering sheep for the Shepherd who longed to have him! So then this thought of constancy keeps company with that of confidence in the mind of the sheep this nightfall; and to them is to be added one further reflection—

AN ATMOSPHERE OF CONTENTMENT

"And I will dwell in the house of the LORD for ever." I don't know whether sheep ever sigh; but, if they do, I can so well imagine that they would settle down to sleep at nightfall with a sigh of contentment. They are home for the night; blessed foregleam of being home forever. All through the day the shepherd had been leading and guiding his flock to the fold where he had prepared a place for them; even as the Master has said (John 14:2–3), "In My Father's house . . . I go to prepare a place for you . . . that where I am, there ye may be also." We often say, "Home's where Mother is"; well, heaven's where Jesus is. And, rest content, where the Shepherd is, the sheep will be.

> We two are so joined,
> He'll not be in Heaven, and leave me behind.

Not all the powers of Satan and hell can dissolve the mighty link that binds me to my Savior, for it is of His, not of my, making. Listen again to the old familiar words of blessed certitude, as He speaks them anew to our grateful hearts: "My sheep . . . shall never perish, neither shall any man pluck them out of My hand" (John 10:27–28). But the devil might, did you say? Nay, "man" is in italics; it is not in the Greek: the truer rendering would be, "neither shall anyone"—man or devil. But they might pluck themselves out, do you think? No, never; for the promise starts by saying, "They shall never perish." Oh, happy contentment for trusting souls!

When we have come to the words, "all the days of my life" we naturally ask, and what then? That is a question to which *philosophy* has no certain answer, a question to which *science* has no answer at all; a question to which *revelation* alone has the true answer. Not that this last has given us a full answer. It begins in Old Testament days with scarcely more than just a hint here and there; but that gradually broadens, until the New Testament revelation of Him who "brought life and immortality to light [Greek, out into the light] through the gospel" (2 Tim. 1:10). Perhaps, if we knew too much of the joys and glories of heaven, our hearts would be so enraptured that it would cut the nerve of our appointed enterprise on earth. Just enough is brought out into the light to fill our hearts with blest anticipation of what lies beyond "all the days of my life." John McNeill tells the story of a village idiot boy, who, though attending day and Sunday school, never showed any sign of ever learning anything. When he came to die, someone went to visit him, and realizing how difficult it would be to help such a one, the friend started repeating to him the Twenty-third Psalm, in their own Scots metrical version. When she had come to the last verse, and had spoken the first two lines,

> *Goodness and mercy all my life*
> *Shall surely follow me,*

she paused from sheer emotion; when, to her intense surprise, the poor, vacant idiot boy—we said he had been through Sunday school—propped himself up on his elbow, and with a gleam in his eyes, as though a great light were breaking, finished the verse—

> *And in God's house for evermore*
> *My dwelling place shall be.*

The effort exhausted him, and he fell back, gone. But, on what a note! My friend, you are no idiot, thank God; but have you the fore-gleam?

We get the word *"dwell"* here, as if the psalmist had in

mind something less transitory, something more permanent than just a stay for the night. The end of every day saw the sheep in a fold on the mountain, but David at this point encourages us to look for the lasting residence beyond. We believers are not at home in this world, we are but passing through "as strangers and pilgrims" (1 Peter 2:11). Nevertheless, our hearts may live across the border even while our feet still tramp this side. May we indeed, in the spirit of Ephesians 2:6, so live "in the heavenlies" all our days now, that we may the more happily enter the heaven itself at day's end. So may these be "days of heaven upon earth."

Let us beware of imagining that the life of heaven will be a lazy life of listless loafing. The revelation about that is that "His servants shall serve Him" (Rev. 22:3). What kind of work we shall do we have not been told, but we do know that whatever its nature we shall be in a condition to do it perfectly. We shall not be hindered as down here by the query whether it is, in reality, of any use, because we shall there understand all its deep value and importance. We shall not be hampered as down here by physical limitations and disabilities; self and nerves and tiredness will not spoil. Have you ever realized that there will be no beds, or bedrooms in heaven? How do I know? Why, because we are told "there shall be no night there" (Rev. 22:5). Night is for sleep and rest, but we shall need none there. We shall be able, without fear of a breakdown, to work on, and on, and on. When we come to "dwell in the house of the LORD," we shall discover that the thrice-blessed members of that royal household have many duties assigned them, much service apportioned. Let us do all we can in His service here that we may, in some sense, thereby be trained for work hereafter.

Two wondrous contentments are to be experienced, in the gathering of the sheep into the fold, "for ever." The first is so amazing as to be almost incredible; we could not have believed it if the Bible had not specifically recorded it—*"He shall see of the travail of His soul, and shall be satisfied"* (Isa. 53:11). When He contemplates all the blood and anguish entailed to bring the sheep home, He shall feel that it has been well worth while. Wonder of wonders! The second is only what we should expect—*"I shall be satisfied, when I awake, with thy likeness"* (Ps. 17:15). He and I satisfied: what contentment!

Here it is, then, our closing meditation and our final situation (a) Personal—"I shall," together with all the true members of the flock. (b) Residential—"dwell in the house of the LORD," with all that is included, implied and involved in that glorious statement. (c) Eternal—"for ever." Amid all the changes and chances of this mortal life we long for permanence; it is inborn within us, as we find in Ecclesiastes 3:11 (margin), "He hath set eternity in their heart." As Dr. F. B. Meyer says, "Our nature is keyed not to the temporal but to the eternal. This present life is all to and fro, and we long to be settled somewhere. Here and in present conditions it is a goodly thing that the sheep "shall go in and out" (John 10:9); but hereafter, they "shall go no more out."

Well, this king, David, has come to the end of his present testimony. Being a one-time shepherd, we are not surprised that he has told his story under the figure of the old life with the sheep; being a poet, he has naturally cast it in poetic form. The imagery, and the artistry, of the thing are bewitching to the sensitive soul; but there is more in it than that—there is all the wonder of intimate reality and relationship between the sheep and the Shepherd; and though perforce the psalmist has had to speak much about himself and what he gets out of that relationship, yet his objective is to show not himself but his Lord. He begins with Him in time (v. 1), "The LORD is . . ."; he ends with Him in eternity (v. 6) ". . . the LORD for ever." And all in between is what David has found Him to be.

I was called just after the close of the 1914 War to see a young fellow who was dying from his war wound. I began by speaking of ordinary things, but soon I turned to the deeper realities; and as I mentioned the Savior's name, the face of the young soldier lit up in a way that I shall never forget as he said, "Sir, He's everything to me." And presently Herbert went fearlessly, even gladly, "through the valley of the shadow of death," for He was with him. Tell me, my reader, you who have companied with me in these simple studies of this lovely Scripture, tell me—how much is He to you? Nothing? Something? Everything?

I close with an oft-told little story. It was a Sunday school tea and prize-giving and the children were giving a concert on their own to the parents and friends. One item on the program was a recitation by a mite in the primary department; and she had been carefully drilled and instructed for the purpose in the Twenty-third Psalm. By the great night, she knew it perfectly; and when the "artistes" forgathered in the platform room she was word-perfect: "The LORD is my Shepherd; I shall not want"—and so on. Then came the big moment; and, full of confidence, the wee maiden appeared in order to say her piece. Alas, the enthusiastic reception of the audience made her nervous; but she began, "The LORD is my Shepherd . . ."—then, a blank! She just couldn't think how it went on. Perhaps you have had a like experience, and can sympathize. She began again, but with no better result; and quite naturally she became tearful. But, before quitting her post, she made one last desperate effort, and getting by then a glimmering of what it should be, before rushing off she gave them her version of the verse—"The LORD is my Shepherd, *that's all I want.*" Ay, that's all!

Chapter Eight

A TASK FOR EACH NEW DAY

"And other sheep I have, which are not of this fold: them also I must bring . . . and there shall be one fold, and one shepherd."—John 10:16.

All the while that I have been writing the foregoing pages, this verse has been constantly intruding itself into my mind, and clamoring for attention. Forgive me, then, if I keep you a few brief moments longer—"I can no other!" Four things leap out at me from this verse, and first—

THE DIVINE PREROGATIVE

"Other sheep I have, which are not of this fold." There is no earthly reason why any one of us should be saved. Quite the contrary, for we are all rebels against the all-holy and almighty God. The only reason for our salvation is a heavenly reason, namely, the sovereign grace of God. It is only because He has decided and designed it that we can be saved—or, to keep to the metaphor of our studies, that we can become His sheep.

Let us never forget that the whole matter of our redemption begins on God's side: that we never could have called Him "my Shepherd," as David did, unless He had first elected to call us "My sheep." But who are these "other sheep" who are "not of this fold"?

Let it be noted, first, that *(a) The one fold is, of course, the Jewish fold.* David himself was of this fold, and all the Old Testament saints, the first disciples of the Master, and most of that early Christian church. That company was a highly privileged one. Out of that fold the Holy Scriptures came, to that fold "the word of this salvation" was first sent. Unfortunately, the Jews fell from their estate; they did not recognize their Shepherd's voice, and they actually cast Him out of His own fold in sad rebellion, for which they have suffered down to this very day, and will suffer till the great day when He shall return to be at last acknowledged as their true Shepherd.

Mark, also, that *(b) The other fold is, of course, the Gentile fold*—in the strict sense of the term. While the Jews imagined that salvation was their own exclusive property, God, to whom, of course, the prerogative properly belonged, had planned far otherwise. His heart was on "the other sheep" as well. That is why those Gentile Greeks of John 12:20, who inquired, "Sir, we would see Jesus," brought the Master such exhilaration of spirit as verse 23 suggests. They belonged to that other fold, were forerunners of those "other sheep" for whom He longed—and here they were, seeking Him. It was in connection with this incident that He said, verse 32, "I, if I be lifted up from the earth, will draw all men unto Me." Not all without exception, of course, for that would have been untrue to the facts; but all without distinction: Gentiles as well as Jews. Here is the means of drawing them: His uplifting on the Cross, as He Himself would have us understand (v. 33); and here is the beginning of drawing them, those Greek inquirers.

Perhaps, before we pass on, we might remind ourselves that

(c) There are many folds comprised within this Gentile fold— there are the brown "sheep" of India, and the yellow "sheep" of China and Japan, and the red "sheep" of South America, and the white "sheep" of Europe, and the black "sheep" of Africa, and the Wilderness of Sin; there are the old sheep and the young lambs—

> *Red and yellow, black and white,*
> *They are precious in His sight,*
> *Jesus died for all the children of the world.*

Yes; how His heart longs after them all; and how our hearts should beat in tune with His, and our purpose fall into line with His. And that brings me to—

THE DIVINE IMPERATIVE

"Them also I must bring." *Must:* that is a strange word to apply to the All-free Almighty, isn't it? Well, this is not the only place where it occurs. Let me remind you of John 3:14, "As Moses lifted up the serpent in the wilderness, even so *must* the Son of Man be lifted up." Must? Yes, if ever we poor sinners are to be saved at all. Or, John 4:4, "He *must* needs go through Samaria." Must? There was a much more popular route to travel north—to cross Jordan, in Judea, to pass up through Perea, and to recross Jordan into Galilee, thus bypassing the country of the Samaritans with whom "the Jews have no dealings." Yes, but if He had gone that way the Lord Jesus would not have met with the needy woman at the well-side. Or, John 9:4. "I *must* work the works of Him that sent Me, while it is day." Must? Indeed; for there was a plan of God in fulfillment of which He had come, and to the perfection of which He was committed. Do you notice that in every case it was the compulsion of love that laid on Him these uttermost necessities? And we might have considered other instances in the course of the Gospels, Luke 19:5, for example.

But we come back to our present passage, to find the same thing. The sight of the needy, hungry crowds that followed Him in that earlier part of His ministry always deeply stirred His heart. "When He saw the multitudes, He was moved with compassion on them, because they . . . were . . . as sheep having no shepherd" (Matt. 9:36). How could these sheep of themselves find food to sustain them? They need a shepherd's providing care. How could these sheep save themselves from the attacks of beasts and bandits? They need a shepherd's protecting care. Pathetic, tragic figures: the Lord, in all His tender concern, says, "Them also I must bring." But how will that be brought to pass? That takes us to the thought of—

THE DIVINE EXECUTIVE

It seems to me that the soul-winning, sheep-finding enterprise is linked up with three things. *(a) the Cross*—"the good shepherd giveth His life for the sheep" (John 10:11). It was the only way: if there had been any other, that bitter cup of Matthew 26:39 would have been withheld from Him; but all the perfect justice of the mighty transaction was wrapped up in His drinking it. This is not the place to discuss the matter; let it only be stated here that so perfectly did the Cross deal with the whole situation, that God would now be unjust if He did not forgive sins, if He did not save sinners, if He did not rescue the "sheep which was lost" (Luke 15:6). On the ground of Calvary He becomes both "just, and the justifier of him which believeth in Jesus" (Rom. 3:26). The Cross is the instrument of our salvation, divinely and eternally planned, and executed in time by Him who was "the lamb slain from the foundation of the world" (Rev. 13:8). He who is the Shepherd was first the Lamb.

The second agency in our salvation is *(b) the Holy Spirit*—who has been described as, for this age, the Executive of the Godhead. If a man is to change from the natural swine to the supernatural sheep, he can never accomplish it by any effort of his own; it can only be done by a rebirth. "Ye must be born again," says the Master (John 3:7); and this time it must be "born of the Spirit" (v. 8). The Christian life is not merely the better life, but the different life. Ordinary, natural life, though it be as good as that of Nicodemus, would be quite out of place in the rarified atmosphere of heaven; it couldn't breathe so far up. If a fish conceived the idea of becoming a man, it could not effect the transmogrification of its own effort—it could, by such means, only make itself a better fish. Except a fish be born again, it cannot enter into the kingdom of man; and "except a man be born again, he cannot see the Kingdom of God."

How obvious is all this to every Bible-taught believer. But there is one other link in the sheep-finding that I want, not only to mention, but to stress just now, for I think this must be the reason why I have been urged in mind to include this further chapter in our studies. This third link is *(c) the Christian.* When, in the Matthew 9 passage that we quoted just now, the Lord referred to the sheep without a shepherd, He went on to impress upon His own that they should pray God "that He will send forth labourers" (v. 38); for it is to us Christians—not to angels, who would jump at the chance—that is committed the great responsibility and immense privilege of trying to reach and touch and fetch the lost for Him. That is the human side of His executive plan for man's salvation. When, in S. D. Gordon's legend, the archangel Gabriel was talking with the ascended Lord, and asked what plans He had left behind for carrying forward the message, he was told that Peter, and James, and John, and Andrew, and the rest of the little company had been entrusted with the task. When further questioned as to what would be done if they failed Him, the Master answered, "I have no other plan." No other—for, as E. M. Bounds said, in one of his books on prayer, "Man is God's method."

How eagerly that little band did press forward with the good news of the Gospel—none more earnest than Peter. To him had been given the promise of "the keys," wherewith to open the door of the Christian flock (Matt. 16:19), and in Acts 2 he did open the door to those from the Jewish fold to pass through when "about three thousand" crowded in to the Good Shepherd's domain. And in Acts 10, he did the same for those who desired to pass through from the Gentile fold and, to the astonishment of the Jews, the "gift" was poured out "on the Gentiles also" (v. 45), those "other sheep." But a like earnestness characterized all of them, for as Mark 16:20 tells us, they went forth and preached everywhere the Lord working with them, and confirming the word with signs following." By the way, we often speak about working for God: don't you think that, in the light of this verse, the better description would be working with God?

What fine enthusiasm, then, they all displayed, in advancing the Shepherd's cause! But what of us? We, by His sovereign grace, through the blood of His cross and the regenerating power of the Spirit, have been brought into all the amazing joys and blessings of those who are His sheep; what have we been doing about "other sheep"? The Shepherd says that He "must" have them; and He has taken us into the partnership of the great business of "bringing" them in. Are we full partners, having put all we've got into the business? Or, are we but sleeping partners—in this case, getting nothing out of it, because we are putting nothing into it? Through Peter's example, He has made this a test of our love for Him: not what we say, but what we do, about this sheep work. "Lovest thou Me . . . ? Yea, Lord . . . Feed my lambs . . . my sheep" (John 21:15–17). Oh, to be all at it—and always at it.

The famous Dean Vaughan, who did so much for the training of young men for the Church of England ministry, used always to give them—his "doves," as they were called—a final charge on the eve of their ordination; and in it, without fail, he always included this piece of precious counsel: "Gentlemen, whatever else you set yourself to accomplish in your new life and work, let it be your earnest endeavor that, as a result of your ministry, when you reach the other side there shall be many who shall come and take you by the hand, and leading you up to the Savior, shall say, 'Lord, this man brought me here.'" Whatever be our ecclesiastical fold, shall we so labor as to have such a reward—the human agent of the Divine Executive? Let us hear, and heed, His loving voice saying to us afresh, "Other sheep . . . I must bring; will you come to help Me fetch them home?"

> *As Thou hast sought, so let me seek,*
> *Thy erring children lost and lone.*

So we think, lastly, of—

THE DIVINE OBJECTIVE

"There shall be one fold, and one Shepherd." I have retained the Authorized Version "fold," because I am quoting; but really it should read, "one flock." Down here, the many folds may still maintain their denominational or other allegiances—Anglican, Methodist, Baptist, Congregationalist, Presbyterian, Roman, Independent, Brethren, or what not— yet, if true believers, all are members of the one flock of God. Up there, the "fold" distinction will disappear, and only the "flock" designation remain. I really don't think it greatly matters in the world what name and uniform we have, so long as they represent differences only of order and form of worship, and so long as they are loyal to truth of fundamental doctrine. After all, different types of worship appeal to differently constituted temperaments. No harm is done to the army by the varieties of regiment, so long as each regiment is loyal to the sovereign and obedient to the king's regulations. But yonder, with all the hedges and barriers down, the sheep of every fold will know glad recognition of each other as true members of the "one flock." Some of the more exclusive brethren will have a great (but then, happy) shock to discover how many names other than theirs are sharing with them the joys of heaven around our "one Shepherd."

That being so, why should we not have more recognition down here of each other's gifts, and service? And, as He prayed (John 17:22) "that they may be one," why should there not, even as there is deep uniformity of the faith we hold, be an evident unity in the love we have for one another, and a fine unanimity of purpose in the service that, together, we render Him? Where could that unity and unanimity be more properly displayed than in a great common adventure in seeking, with Him, to "bring" in those "other sheep" into the "one flock" of the "one Shepherd"?

I bid you, my readers, farewell! May our Shepherd-finding lead us on, and lead us out, into sheep-finding.